A Hair Raising Blowout

by

Constance Barker

Chapter 1

Turning my key in the front door lock of the salon on Monday morning, I looked down at the little girl who had come up beside me. I scanned the sidewalk in both directions looking for her mother and thought out loud, "Knockemstiff, Louisiana, is safe enough for a six-year-old to wander about in by herself, I suppose." I looked at the scattering of broken glass a few shops down the street. "Or it was safe enough until last night."

"Six and a half," insisted the girl.

"Half what?" I said, looking down again at the little blond head.

"Six and a half," she repeated. "I'm six and a half years old as of last Wednesday."

"You had a half birthday and didn't invite me?" I asked.

The word "But" began to form on the girl's face, which shifted immediately into a wry smile. At six and a half, Sarah Jameson already had a fine appreciation of the absurd — a handy talent for getting along in Knockemstiff.

"Mama wonders if you could cut her hair today. She says she is desperate to get her hair cut, desperate with a capital D. I don't know why it's a capital D, if it's not the beginning of a sentence, but that's what she says."

"I believe I can, Sarah, but let me check my book." I swung the door open and let us both into the Teasen and Pleasen Hair Salon. "Why didn't your mother call on the phone to make an appointment?"

"Daddy's been on the phone hollerin' for the past hour. He woke me up yelling 'What?' and 'Damn,' over and over. So Mama sent me down here to ask could she get her hair cut with a capital D."

"OK, let's see," I said looking at my appointment book. "And Sarah," I said absently, "nice young ladies don't say 'damn.'"

"That's exactly what Mama says. I don't think Daddy is setting a good example for me. Some days all he says is 'damn' all day." She pursed her lips. "To tell you the truth," she said, "this is looking like one of those days."

I had been about to tell Sarah to send her mother over at 3:15 that afternoon, when I had an opening, but on second thought I said, "Tell your mother to come on over, Sarah. I'll work her in right away."

"My daddy says you work her *over*," observed Sarah. "Mama comes home from here, and he yells, 'Damn, what happened to your head? Has that woman worked you over again?' Then they discuss the haircut and whatever else is on their minds, I guess."

I took a lollipop from the bowl on the counter and handed it down to her. "Would you like a purple one, Sarah?"

"Yes, thank you, Miz Jefferies."

"Go tell your mother to come around directly with a capital D, OK?"

As I was seeing Sarah out the door, I saw the slight form of Annie Simmerson coming along the sidewalk. "Annie," I called out, "are you on your way to work?"

"Well, good morning, Savannah," Annie said, and looking down, "Good morning, Sarah." Sarah put her hand out and Annie shook it solemnly.

Annie turned back to me. "I'm on my way to Dr. Cason's office, yes." Annie worked as a secretary and assistant at the general practitioner's office here in Knockemstiff. When you saw her on the street, she was always wearing a charcoal blazer, pressed white blouse and some flavor of slacks that would go with the pink lab coat she wore at work. She was only 25 but seemed older. Everyone loved her because she always had a radiant smile and a kind word, so I knew Sarah would be OK with Annie as an escort.

"Would you mind walking Sarah around the block to her apartment building?"

"I'd be delighted to do that on this fine sunny day, Savannah." A sunny day in June meant that Knockemstiff would be oppressively hot. It was only 76 at this time of the morning, though, so a person determined to have a positive attitude could see the day as fine.

"Sarah honey," I said, "how about if Miss Simmerson walks you home?"

Sarah frowned. She whispered to me, "Do I have to share my lollipop?"

I stepped back into the shop and pulled an orange lollipop out of the bowl for Annie and shooed them both down the sidewalk. "Miss Simmerson has her own lollipop. You two go on."

"Yes Ma'am."

Sarah skipped down the sidewalk, with the lollipop in one hand and her other hand held by Annie. Annie skipped a few steps herself, causing her brown curls to bounce. She slowed her walk so she could peer into the shop that had the smashed window, as Mr.

Keshian came out of the shop with a broom. I could see him telling Annie about the window with that quiet intense way he has. Though I could not hear what he was saying, I could see Annie listening patiently and nodding. That was Annie, always taking time to express concern for other people's problems. No trouble was too small for her attention.

The phone was ringing in the salon, so I went back in and picked it up to hear a raspy woman's voice in full flow as soon as I lifted the phone from the cradle. The voice was in the middle of explaining how to season a cast iron skillet. "Let it bake in a 450 degree oven for half an hour," the voice finished.

I added, "Do that process three or four times to make sure you've got a good finish."

"Oh," said the voice, "I didn't realize you'd picked up, Savannah. Is this Savannah?"

I plucked one of my cards from the plastic holder on the counter and peered at it. "Savannah Jefferies," I read out loud. "That's what it says on my card."

"Oh, Savannah, this is Dolores."

While I was busy thinking, *Yes, I know it's Dolores*, I walked over to get the coffee pot going. She continued without a pause to tell me about how her niece Julia had simmered jambalaya in her biggest cast iron skillet, the one Dolores inherited from her grandmother, and then scraped it out with a stainless steel scrub thingy. And that boyfriend of hers. And why couldn't Emmit do something? And what's going on with that broken window at the Paramabet place where they sell the funny étouffée?

And she was about to rattle on to another topic when I said, "Broken window?"

"Oh, Savannah, the broken window at the Paramabet place just three blocks from you. Haven't you heard?"

"No, Dolores. What happened?"

"Oh, Savannah, the window of the shop," she rasped dramatically, "was broken." Dolores paused for effect. The only time Dolores Pettigrew ever paused was for effect.

"Dolores, when did this happen?"

"Oh, Savannah, Emmit told me about it on Sunday after services."

So it must have happened Saturday night, I thought, and said aloud, "And Mr. Keshian's window was broken Sunday night."

"Oh, Savannah, the cobbler? Mr. Keshian the cobbler on your block? Oh dear. So we have a cluster of window breakings!" She paused.

"Dolores, two isn't much of a cluster." But she made a valid point. Two broken windows in one weekend was a crime wave for Knockemstiff, population 772, not counting the many people scattered around the countryside and the residents of the little knot of civilization that had grown up around the Interstate exit in recent decades.

Dolores was moving into the "Honestly, I don't know what the world is coming to" phase of her observations when Nellie Phlint came through the front door of the hair salon, ready for her first client at 10:00 am. I took the opportunity to break into Dolores' overview of today's moral turpitude with, "Oh, Dolores, sorry; Nellie just came in. Let me talk to you later? Thanks for the news about the window." After another 10 minutes of additional Dolores observations and secondary, tertiary, and further good-byes (What comes after tertiary?) on my part, I got Dolores to wind down sufficiently to hang up.

I kept my hand on the phone, and it rang a few seconds later. When I picked it up, that raspy voice was already talking, this time about frying chicken, and when I heard Dolores' niece replying in the background, I took the opportunity to say, "Dolores, will you be a little late for your appointment today?"

"Oh, Savannah, is that you? Say again?"

"Will you be a little late for your appointment today?"

"Oh, Savannah, *yes*. My niece Julia can't drop me off until a quarter past 11 on account of her little boy. Did you hear about that already? You're one of the best-informed people I know." I was curious about what was happening with Julia's little boy but thought it best not to ask. By the time I hung up the phone again, the coffee was perked.

"Dolores will be a little late for her appointment," I called out to Nellie Phlint, who was in the back room looking for something.

"I've got her down for a quarter past 11," she called back.

"Yep," I said. We all expected Dolores about a quarter of an hour behind whatever time Dolores thought she was supposed to be there. Dolores was quite punctual if you reset your expectations by a quarter of an hour.

Nellie came out of the back room with a box of emery boards and orange sticks. She is the beautician at the Teasen and Pleasen, mainly doing nails, make-up and hair coloring.

"Did you have a nice weekend?" I asked over the rim of my coffee mug.

"Where to start…" She plopped down the box at her station, put both of her immaculately manicured hands on the little table, and twisted her head to look at me sideways. "That Rudy! It's not enough that he drinks to excess on a Saturday night with those loud friends of his from the sawmill, he's got to come home and wake up the kids to go bustling out into the woods to see some unusual owl he's just heard."

"The swamp by your house, you mean?"

"Those woods, yes." Nellie lowered her forehead to the edge of the table. With her pixie cut, she looked like Peter Pan had crash landed — a Peter Pan who had moved out of Neverland long ago.

"You can just picture the bunch of them out in the swamp in the pitch dark looking for a bird that's hooting up in a tree somewhere, can't you? Well, it was exactly what you would expect, except none of the injuries was serious."

Nellie's husband and three boys had found no place in the natural world that they did not like and no season in which they did not like to go there. Nellie kept up with them as best she could, serving as safety officer as far as possible, which usually meant binding wounds and transporting injured parties to the Quick Help doc-in-a-box clinic over by the Interstate. Rudy and the three boys were some of the clinic's best customers.

Nellie would rather have stayed home watching TV, but she figured that being outdoors with her husband more or less sober was better than having him off with his no-good friends, not all of whom were male. As a result of the outdoor activities, Nellie was a lean, strong, slightly weather-beaten woman, yet she somehow managed to maintain her manicure. I had never understood how she did that, and now I wondered how she had kept up with the boys in the swamp.

"Goodness, Nellie," I said. "Were you hurt?"

She straightened up. "I'm fine, Savannah. I didn't go into the woods with them. I stood at the edge of the trees with a flashlight so they could find their way out again. Otherwise, they'd still be in there. Did I mention he took his deer rifle into the woods 'for protection'?"

"Oh dear."

"I said, 'Rudy, what is there in the woods next to our house that you need protection from?'"

"He said, 'Nellie, there's creatures in this world that don't deserve to live.'"

"'Creatures?' I yelled at him. 'There's no creatures in our woods.' Which is not strictly true, but there's hardly any gators anymore and nothing else you'd use a thirty-ought-six on. By this time they're all tramping into the swamp."

"He yells back at me over his shoulder, 'Two-legged creatures, Nellie. They could be lurking anywhere with evil intent.'"

"So they're thrashing around in there, and I never hear the owl again with all this commotion going on, but pretty soon I hear Rudy swear, and the boys all yell, 'Daddy, are you OK?' And it turns out he tripped over a root and twisted his ankle. The two older boys help him out of the woods, and bringing up the rear is my youngest, Dale, struggling along with that thirty-ought-six tucked under his arm like he's going jousting with it, and the business end is pointed more or less in the direction of his father and brothers. I was praying the safety was on. I got over to take the rifle from Dale as quick as I could. The safety was on, and when I went to unload the gun later, I found it was never loaded the whole time. So that was good."

"You know how to unload Rudy's deer rifle?"

"Oh, yes, Savannah. Rudy insisted that I learn to handle that gun years ago 'for protection.' Anyway, I paid close attention to the deer rifle lessons so I would know how to unload the thing. I've probably unloaded that gun more times than anybody has unloaded a thirty-ought-six throughout history."

She put her forehead back down on the table. "I'm too old for this."

"Nellie, you're only 42."

"Are you sure? It feels like more. I'm going to check my ID." She rummaged around in her purse. I handed her a cup of coffee. Eventually she pulled out a bottle of ibuprofen, shook out several tablets without looking, and swallowed them with a gulp of coffee. This is what passes for drug abuse in Knockemstiff.

I've known Nellie since we were both children. She dreamed of becoming a stylist for the rich and famous in Baton Rouge or maybe even New Orleans. Life didn't turn out that way, thanks to the careless conclusion of one of their dates in the cab of Rudy's pickup. ("I did at least enjoy it," Nellie reported.) Rudy was her high school sweetheart, and she married him a few months ahead of the arrival of the first of their three boys.

Nellie's 10 o'clock came in, along with the other two stylists who work at the salon, Betina Levesque and Pete Dawson. They made a nice looking couple, even though they were not a "couple." Betina had eyes only for other men, and Pete had eyes only for other men also, a fact that he didn't hide, but he was so shy, he'd never had a serious boyfriend. He lived vicariously through Betina's stories of the studly males she dated, and she had dated a lot of studly males. And brought back a lot of stories.

A stunning redhead, Betina was wearing her usual little summer dress with flowers on it. (Her concession to winter was to put a coat over the cotton dress.) Betina was one of those girls who's thoughtlessly sexy. I'd often see her leaning up against her male clients in alluring ways. It wasn't as if she didn't know the effect she had on these men. But if she thought about it at all, she must have thought that this was the way a girl was supposed to get along with males of the species. Betina was a lovely person through and through, though Pete sometimes cringed at the casual way she dismissed her suitors. In the two years since finishing high school, Betina had had maybe one relationship that lasted more than four months. We heard all about her exploits on Monday mornings.

Pete couldn't understand where she found these men. "How many good-looking 20-somethings could there be in a town this size?" he asked.

Betina would toss her head and explain that if the domestic market could not support the local demand, a girl just had to import what she needed. As she trimmed the shoulder-length hair of her first client of the day, she said, "Why, just this weekend I was entertained by a nice young man from Studlyville." That was what she called the nearby town of Stanleyville that was home to a large oil refinery. "He took me to dinner at the Studlyville Hotel, and we went to see a movie at the State Theatre."

"What movie did you see?" Pete asked. He always asked what movie Betina saw because it amused him to hear that she had no idea.

"It had some shooting and explosions. Helicopter gunships. And that hunky guy from the jungle commando movie that was out last summer. You know the one I mean? I don't recall the name of it. It was so exciting."

"So you like this guy? Is he super-studly?" Pete asked.

"Does he have a brain?" Nellie added.

"He's studly enough to make a movie exciting, I guess," Betina said. "And I'll have you know," she said with her green eyes flashing in a good-natured way in Nellie's direction, "that he's thinking about going to the junior college over in Paudy to study oil refining."

Sarah's mother, Bee, came in at this point, chatting with Annie, and I remembered that Annie had an appointment with Pete for a trim. They both went over to the "café" area of the salon. We keep an urn of coffee going and put pastries out. People leave payment for the pastries in an honor-system basket. I could see that Annie was sympathizing with something Bee said. Annie dropped a couple of dollars in the basket and then dropped in a couple more for Bee's Danish.

Meanwhile, Betina was carrying on with her date drama. Pete was urging her to further specifics, which we all considered part of his Monday-morning duties.

Betina said, "You remember what Zac Ephron looked like in Hairspray? He looks kinda like that, and he does dress nicely for a guy who works at an oil refinery." She stopped trimming her client's bangs and got a distant look in her eyes. "He has a really cute tongue," she said.

Both Pete and Betina's client let out little moan-like noises. In the eight months since Betina started working at the salon, I've noticed a significant upswing in Monday-morning business. The clients scheduled for later in the morning tended to come in early and enjoy cups of coffee and Betina tales until their appointment times rolled around.

No hurry.

We all carried on in this leisurely way until 11:14, when we were surprised to see Dolores Pettigrew coming in breathlessly a minute early, exclaiming about a windshield even before she had the front door of the salon open. "I've never seen the like of it," she concluded, standing in the doorway, "in our little town."

"Good morning, Dolores," I said. "The like of what?"

"Oh, good morning, Savannah. The like of August Anderson's windshield."

Betina's head came around. "August's windshield? What's going on?"

August was a close friend of Betina's, equally pretty but as shy and reserved as she could possibly be, so August did not have the male following that Betina enjoyed.

"Oh, Betina," Dolores gasped, "I just heard it directly from the Bald Eagle."

The Bald Eagle, Sanders Bloomington was a 72-year old widower who was almost entirely bald. He had appeared in the doorway behind Dolores exactly on time for his regular weekly appointment with Betina. Suddenly it was clear why Dolores was one minute early: She got here just in time to upstage the Eagle's news.

Except that we hadn't understood what she was talking about, so as Sanders came in the salon we all stared at him and waited.

He looked around at our expectant faces. "I see you've heard the news."

"What happened, Sanders?" I asked.

"This morning I got up at 5:30 to go to my sky diving class and saw the windshield of August Anderson's Toyota in the driveway next door."

"It was smashed?" I asked.

"Oh, no," he said. "Somebody had spray-painted the word "SLUT" on the windshield in big red letters."

Chapter 2

In some places and for some people, having SLUT painted on their windshield would be regarded as an annoying prank. The worst part would be scraping the paint off.

But Knockemstiff was still a quiet, conservative town, and August Anderson was a quiet, conservative young woman. She would take the painted "verdict" as a stain on her character. She would think that's what people must think of her. As Betina said in the silence that followed the Bald Eagle's description of the incident, "August will be mortified."

No one who visited the salon that day could come up with any reason why someone would paint SLUT on August's windshield. No one could think of any reason to be jealous of August. Sure, August was as pretty as any girl in town, but she was threatening no one's relationship with anyone. Betina was certain of that.

The irony was, August wasn't a slut. As Betina pointed out, if August had had even one relationship that went beyond a serious kiss, she would not take the slut thing so seriously.

Betina had tried to match up August with any number of boys, but August usually resisted. They had double-dated a few times. Betina was sure that all of August's double-date guys (as well as one of the guys who was supposed to be Betina's date) had asked August out afterwards. August had gone out with one of those guys, maybe a couple of times. That was about it.

That meant that August had refused dates with a number of guys. Could one of them be upset enough to want to embarrass her? Betina couldn't imagine this was the case. But try as we did, we couldn't come up with a better explanation.

The smashed windows also remained mysterious. Someone who talked to Mr. Keshian, maybe it was Annie Simmerson, said that he had found a brass cherub on the floor of his shop. It looked like a paperweight. Someone apparently threw it at his window.

No one could think of any reason to dislike Mr. Keshian. He'd been a cobbler in Knockemstiff for nearly two decades, and he did excellent work on shoes, handbags, belts — anything leather. He'd never been known to cheat anyone. In fact, several people who lived on limited incomes said that he had made repairs for them and would not accept a cent in payment. Who would want to harm such a person? In fact, all the victims of these crimes and pranks were upstanding citizens, so who in the heck was targetting them. And was I next? Somebody wrote SLUT on my windshield they'd get slapped into next week.

After I had blow-dried my last head of hair on Monday, I walked home by way of the shop run by the Paramabets. They have been in Knockemstiff far longer than Mr. Keshian. A couple of generations of Paramabets have offered various types of take-out food from the same shop for as long as I can remember. Their most popular items were tacos. I have no idea how people from Delhi became taco masters, but they were famous for making the best tacos in this half of Louisiana, not that they had a lot of competition. They also sold an Indian flat bread called nan that everybody liked and a dish they called étouffée, but that some observed was actually crawdad and okra curry.

I don't know a curry from a surrey, but I loved the étouffée and stopped at the Paramabets at least once a week for take-out food. This looked like a good time to walk by and take a look at their smashed window. The thundershowers that had passed through briefly in the afternoon cooled off the temperature a few degrees. The rain steamed on the hot streets, though, sending the humidity even higher than it'd already been. The air smelled steamy and metallic. My sleeveless top was already clinging to me before I was halfway down the block.

When I got there, Connor O'Sullivan was removing the last of the broken glass and window frame from the front of the Paramabet's shop. Connor is a third-generation blacksmith who makes everything from spiral staircases to small sculptures he calls "iron poems." He wrote poems in words as well, and often read them aloud on open-mic nights at the Knockemback Tavern in town.

Tonight, though, Connor was plying his sideline trade as a glazier. Connor's father had seen that blacksmithing did not occupy a "growing market niche" and apprenticed the teenage Connor to an expert glazier for a few years. This was back in the town of Kilkeedy, Ireland. Connor says that the town was close enough to Limerick to make him a poet but not close enough to make him write limericks.

I was fond of Connor and delighted to see him there. "How goes it, Connor?" I said as I walked up behind him.

I got the impression that he stiffened slightly at the sound of my voice, but he turned around with his usual, "Top o' the evening to ya, Savannah" — the Irish cliché that amused us both. Though he'd never outgrown his Irish accent, he only used Irishisms for amusement. Tonight he didn't sound amused. He had tiny shards of glass in his flaming red beard that glittered in the light from the Paramabet's shop.

"Glazing got you down, Connor?"

"It's bad business this."

I peered into the shop and waved at one of the younger Paramabets behind the counter. "Are they pretty upset by the whole thing?"

"Less upset than they have a right to be, I'd say. The grandfather told me that this is simply karma for some past misdeed." He shook his head. "It's the work of a first-class rascal, if you ask me. They threw this at the window."

He handed me a brass paperweight of an angel as big as his fist.

"Mr. Keshian found a brass paperweight in his shop, too."

"Look at this." He pointed to the little parking area next to the shop where he'd arranged several of the larger pieces of broken glass on the gravel. Following his finger moving across the pieces of glass I saw that someone had spray-painted letters on the window before it was broken. He traced out SL on the left and skipped to the right, where he traced out an E.

"The pieces in the middle are mostly too small to deal with, but if you look at the bigger pieces here and here, we can guess there was an IM there."

"SLIME?" My stomach turned over. "These people have lived here for ages, and I've never heard an unkind word uttered about them." Then I thought about the spray paint on August's windshield and the other broken window. "Oh no," I said, "I wonder if Mr. Keshian's window was spray painted too."

"I'll put in a new window for him tomorrow, and I'd just as soon not know about any more spray painting."

I agreed with him and told him that Mr. Keshian had swept up the glass. But as I was going in to get my food, I was already wondering if Mr. Keshian had dumped the shards into the dumpster behind his shop.

With an order of étouffée and two pieces of flat bread, I walked home deep in thought, no longer hungry. What was happening to Knockemstiff? I grew up here. I had married at 22 and moved to Baton Rouge with my husband. When the marriage fell apart after a few years, I moved back to Knockemstiff because I liked the quiet friendliness of the place.

Literally a backwater, the town of Knockemstiff, Richwater Parish, is on a bayou that was left to its own devices a couple hundred years ago when a branch of the Atchafalaya River decided to move its business 40 miles to the east. That fickle river has changed course every few hundred years since the dawn of time. When part of the river silted up, it found an easier course to the east. As the river flowed merrily off to someplace else, it left behind old sections that still have water in them, some of them flowing this way and that, some of them stagnant and swampy. These river-shaped sections of water are bayous. One of the stagnant, partly swampy sections is the Knockemstiff Bayou.

Some of the old guys who owned shacks on the Knockemstiff Bayou predicted that the river would change back again. "This property'll be worth something again," they'd cackle. "You'll see. Give it another hundred years."

Meanwhile, the oil refinery in Stanleyville had brought in a number of outside influences. People came in from elsewhere, not all of them roustabouts. By and large, though, Knockemstiff remained a quaint world unto itself.

We had seen isolated incidents of spray painting before, but everyone figured it was teenagers acting out. Now that I thought about it, some of the things that had been painted before were a bit mean; not the artistic tags you would expect from teens. None of the earlier spray painting had been as nasty as SLIME and SLUT.

By the time I got home, I had made up my mind to see if I could find out if Mr. Keshian's window had been painted. I put the étouffée in the fridge and called Nellie to ask if she would help me.

"You're inviting me to go dumpster diving for broken glass in the dark?"

"Ahhh, yes, that's about right," I said, then added "I have a good flashlight."

"I too have a good flashlight. So it won't be entirely dark. Good. Excellent. Here's another thought: Let's pass this idea to the police and let them do the diving."

"The Knockemstiff police?"

"You make a good point," she admitted.

"Nellie, I think this needs to be done, and we're the only ones who can do it."

"How did I get to be one of the only ones who can do it?" she wondered.

"Nellie, this is the same dumpster we use for the salon, and you know your way around in there."

She barked a rueful laugh. Nellie had closed up the salon for me one evening and accidentally tossed out the day's receipts with the hair clippings and other trash instead of taking the money to the bank. We hadn't realized it for a couple of days. Fortunately, the dumpster had not been emptied. Nellie dug through a lot of rubbish in that dumpster to find the money. Pete had been gentlemanly enough to climb in and help her, though he also delighted in referring to the dumpster forever after as the "night depository."

"Bring some gloves," I added.

Half an hour later I was peering into the dumpster when Nellie walked up with a flashlight that looked like a car's headlight.

"Your flashlight is way better than mine," I said with admiration. "What else have you got there? Is that a rifle?"

"Rudy made me bring it for protection."

"I feel safer already."

"I also have a first aid kit," she said hefting a large suitcase. "Just the normal items of a mother with three boys."

"Safer and safer," I said. "I looked in the dumpster while I was waiting, and I think some of the pieces are pretty big. They're over on the right side."

We climbed in the left side and started hefting the jagged pieces of glass so we could get a good look. Right away we saw red spray paint on some pieces and put those aside.

"Hop out, and I'll hand the painted ones to you."

In less than an hour we had only cut ourselves once apiece and had put together enough pieces of glass to make out SH. Then I found a big piece with most of a T.

"I'll bet we can guess the letter in the middle."

"Yeah," Nellie said. "Part of the SLUT SLIME series. Collect them all. Win a prize."

We wrapped the pieces of glass in newspaper and stashed them in the salon's back room in case they were needed as evidence. I helped Nellie carry all the stuff she'd brought back to her place. She thanked me for including her.

I was exhausted. Now that I was walking alone, it was kind of creepy knowing that someone out there had mean intentions and was willing to smash things. What if I bumped into this person? What I did see around the corner surprised me even more. Lying on the grass was a small shape in a white dress, as if a little angel had crashed on the lawn. I ran over and shone my flashlight on her face. Sarah! I bent down over her, shouting her name.

Her eyes popped open, and she screamed in my face, thrashing to get away.

"Zombie! Zombie!" she shouted.

"It's Savannah, honey. Calm down. Are you OK?"

She lay still on the grass. "Oh," she said. She sat up. "You don't smell so good. I thought you were one of the undead."

"Mmm, I wrangled with a dumpster tonight. How come you're sleeping on the lawn?" The white angel dress was actually a terrycloth robe, I saw now.

"I was looking at the Milky Way. Must have fallen asleep. Can't a girl even take a nap without people shouting?"

I could hear her parents inside the apartment building arguing loudly. They hadn't even noticed her scream.

"Sorry I woke you." I sat down next to her, noticing the object lying in the grass that was almost as big as she was. I picked it up. "Is this your rifle?"

"It's Daddy's thirty-ought-six," she explained. "I unloaded it, but it's not a toy to be played with." She took it from me and placed it carefully on the other side of her.

"Do you carry it around for protection?" I asked.

"Protection from what?" she asked.

"Um, I don't know," I said. "What are you doing with it out here?"

"I brought it out here while Daddy and Mama are discussing her manicure and the red dress she bought over in Stanleyville. It's really pretty. Daddy started wondering where she might be going in that dress, only he called it a 'fancy get-up.' 'Where you think you're going in that fancy get-up?' he said. 'That ain't no church outfit.' Then he started speculating about where she might be going. When he starts speculating like that, I think it's a good idea to take the thirty-ought-six someplace else."

"I see what you mean."

The earth under the grass was still damp from the rain, but in a hot, humid climate like this, you get used to being damp one way or another. "It's nice out here, isn't it?" I said, looking up at the sky. The rain clouds had mostly passed, and the sky was decorated with a brilliant spray of stars. A bright sliver of moon was hanging in the west.

Sarah nodded in the dark.

Sarah's mother had told me at the salon that morning that Sarah had arrived home crying. The encounter with Mr. Keshian must have upset her. "Sarah, you remember this morning when you came to the salon?"

She nodded again and hugged her knees to her chest.

"What did you think of all that broken glass at Mr. Keshian's?"

"He was very upset," she said. "It made me think how upset my daddy gets if I break a glass." She shifted to her gruff daddy voice. "'Can't you be more careful, Sarah?' he says." She shrugged. "I guess I can, actually. Anyway, Mr. Keshian was mad at whoever broke his window."

"Did that make you sad?"

"Well, mad, really. At first I was scared, since Mr. Keshian was so upset. Miss Simmerson asked him did he know who might have broken his window. He gave us an angry look. The way he was talking, it was like he thought I broke his window. Miss Simmerson said that it must be hard for him, since he doesn't make very much money with his shop. She was very sympathetic. She said it must be terrible to know that people in town don't like him."

"Annie said that people don't like Mr. Keshian?"

"Was that wrong? Why would someone break Mr. Keshian's window if they like him?"

I was about to ask Sarah to tell me exactly what Annie had said but stopped. Sarah is quite a talker for a six-year-old (or even a six-and-a-half-year-old). Still, exact quotes were asking too much.

"There might be one person who doesn't like Mr. Keshian. Or maybe someone just felt like breaking a window, and Mr. Keshian's was the first one they saw."

Sarah looked at me dubiously. "Why would somebody just feel like breaking a window? People know they're not supposed to break windows."

I was at a loss to explain random mischief myself. "It is mysterious, isn't it? People seem to do things for no reason. It's like that little boy who lives around the corner from you. Tommy? The other day he took your scooter and rode it into a hole in the street so that the wheel broke?"

"That's not mysterious, Miz Jefferies," she said with some exasperation. "I know why he did that. It's because he's an idiot."

"That does explain a lot."

"Maybe somebody broke Mr. Keshian's window because they're an idiot."

"I think we've solved the mystery, Sarah."

I wanted to ask more questions, but it was late, and the argument in the apartment building had gone quiet. "Bed time for all young ladies, I think." I stood up and brushed the grass off my pants — a futile gesture for pants that had been dumpster-diving.

"Good night, Miz Jefferies." She said. She hefted the rifle into her arms, being careful to keep it pointed at the ground a foot or so in front of her, and marched off toward the apartment building.

"Sweet dreams, Sarah."

Time for me to catch up with a bath tub and that plastic container of étouffée.

But the day that began with Sarah and then Annie would end with Sarah and then Annie. Standing against the mulberry tree at the far corner of my backyard, I saw Annie talking into a smart phone. I could only see her because the phone was lighting her face.

This behavior might have been strange in another town. In Knockemstiff, cell phone reception was so spotty that most people did not bother to own one. I got a smart phone years ago because I thought it would allow me to run errands and stay in touch with the salon. But I didn't have coverage around my house, at least not anywhere closer than the mulberry tree, and couldn't get a reliable signal in very many other places, so I rarely turned the phone on.

People who did use cell phones in Knockemstiff could be seen wandering in random directions with their phones held aloft to catch a stray signal. I had once seen someone else standing by my mulberry tree with a phone, so I knew it must be a spot where the signal usually came through. Do mulberries attract cell phone signals?

The strange thing about it was the time. It was nearly midnight, so I was curious about who she could be yakking with at this hour. I think of myself as curious rather than snoopy, so it didn't occur to me to sneak over and eavesdrop. In any case, sneaking up on people is impractical when you smell like a dumpster. If only I had heard what was going on, things might have turned out differently.

Chapter 3

No one saw August on Monday or Tuesday. She called in sick at the Marshé Grosri food mart, according to the cashier who filled in for her. (This store with the Creole name was founded by a Cajun family, possibly back when the river still flowed by here.)

Betina managed to get August on the phone once. August refused to go shopping — either on or off the Internet — or come to the salon for a manicure, the two most therapeutic activities Betina could think of. Betina said that August mostly said things like "What must my mother think of me?" and "Who would do such a thing?"

When Betina told us about the conversation, she reported matter of factly that she had told August, "Being a slut doesn't seem so bad. Why, after high school, I thought of moving to Baton Rouge and giving it a try myself. Just the thought of wearing tiny little skirts and having men trailing along behind me with their tongues hanging out makes me want to go out and buy new shoes."

Apparently that didn't help. "In fact," Betina said, "that was when she started to cry."

Betina sighed and looked down at the floor. "I guess I'm not a very good counselor." She went back to cutting hair, completely oblivious to the mouths that had fallen open at her casual admission she had entertained the thought of going for a slut lifestyle.

It's funny that until then, none of us (with the possible exception of the Bald Eagle) had thought of Betina that way. She wore little sexy dresses, but they weren't *that* little, and they weren't *that* sexy. Mostly. OK, now that Betina had opened the topic, some of her outfits were leaning up against slutty the way she leaned up against some of her clients. All in good fun, right? Eaashhh!

The salon crowd would have liked to discuss the slut concept in much greater detail but felt constrained by Betina's presence. I don't think they needed to feel constrained, since Betina was so forthright about her thoughts on the subject.

I was just as glad to drop the discussion, and made a mental note to have a chat with Betina about the way she came across. Not everyone would think it was all in good fun. As my daddy used to tell me, "When you cast your lure in the bayou, you catch whatever bites."

He meant this as a warning to me, an overview of his philosophy of life, and a come-on for my mother. If my mother was around when he said this, she would say something like, "I caught you by the bayou, didn't I? Let this be a lesson to you, Savannah. Be real careful where you cast your lure. You might catch something you don't want to invite home to dinner." Then she would pretend to cast a lure in my daddy's direction, and he would pretend to be reeled in until she netted him in her arms and subdued his fishy wiggles with wiggles of her own and a series of increasingly affectionate kisses. The fishy wiggles would become a dance around the room.

When I was little, I would roll my eyes at this performance and hope with all my might that none of my neighborhood friends would see it. Then one day when I was about Sarah's age my worst fears were realized. My parents launched into their fishing pantomime, and I could not distract the little friend who was sitting on the floor of our living room. She held the doll we had been playing with and gaped at the performance.

I knew that life as I had known it was over. I was mentally packing my belongings in preparation for running away to Paudy. My parents' performance reached its inevitable conclusion, in which they disappeared down the hall. My friend and I heard the bedroom door close.

Before I could bury my head under a sofa pillow, my friend threw her head back and said, "Savannah! Your parents are so sweet! You are so lucky."

I think I said something clever like "Really?"

"My parents act like they hardly know each other. At least, that's how they act when they're getting along. It's hard to understand how my daddy ever got close enough to my mama to plant the seed that made me."

I'm sure I blushed down to my toes, back up to the top of my head, and down to my toes again. My parents were open in their affections, yet I was embarrassed by them. My friend's parents rarely showed affection, yet she was an avid admirer of "the whole birds-and-bees thing," as she called it.

I eventually came around to my friend's point of view, but I always remembered the cautionary aspect of my father's words. "When you cast your lure in the bayou, you catch whatever bites."

Now I wondered what Betina would make of his country wisdom. Betina seemed to think of herself as a city girl who's in a country bubble that will eventually pop, and she'll magically find herself living in a town large enough to have a shopping mall. In the meantime, she floated above the surface of Knockemstiff without letting much of it get on her.

Betina had thought of me as a sort of substitute mother since her own parents left to homestead in Alaska. A couple of days after Betina graduated from high school, her parents drove off in their over-loaded SUV. She wasn't sure whenever she might see them again.

When Nellie's husband Rudy heard about this move to Alaska, he thought it was the best idea he'd ever heard of. He wanted to load up their truck *right* now and *go*. He thought the wilderness would be perfect for them. By that he meant a different wilderness than the one they already lived in.

Rudy raved about Alaska endlessly and even began reading books about how to tan the hides of small mammals and make jerky. Nellie found this remarkable because "Rudy has not read more than a half dozen books in his entire life." She let him play out his Alaska fascination for a while without much comment. Then one day when Rudy's mother was visiting, Nellie mentioned offhandedly to Mrs. Phlint that Alaska seemed like a good option for the family since alcohol would be hard to come by. Rudy's Alaska ambitions quietly faded away. No doubt Momma had something to do with that.

In the salon, we had more people than usual hanging around in the café area. Pete was going to the Marshé Grosri two or three times a day to restock our pastry supply.

Everyone wanted to discuss August. Everyone knew August, of course. She had grown up in Knockemstiff and been Betina's shadow since grade school. As I said, the two girls were always about equally attractive, but where Betina's figure was dramatic and her personality outgoing, August was willowy and shy. As Betina began dating in high school and became a cheerleader, August mostly watched her friend's romantic adventures from the sidelines.

All day we talked about ways to convince August that the situation was not as bad as she seemed to think. We tried to come up with some way to convince her to consider the SLUT painting a bad joke. Someone said we should tell her that whoever painted her windshield was badly in need of psychiatric care and "some of those psychoprofen meds."

Everybody thought the meds idea was good.

"August's the one who needs the meds," someone added. "How about some happy pills for her?"

"Aw, August just needs to knock back a couple of stiff drinks and forget about it," said another tongue waggler.

In its own way, this comment got to the heart of the matter. Whichever way we looked at it, August's reaction seemed overdone, even for a shy, conservative person. The truth was that we couldn't understand why she was taking it so hard.

Along with the August SLUT issue as a topic of conversation, people in the salon talked about who could have done the spray painting and broken the two shop windows. Hour by hour, as people came and went, this discussion always went through the following points in this order:

1. Who could have done such a thing?

2. Maybe someone doesn't like people who seem foreign.

3. But August isn't foreign.

4. Who could have done such a thing?

It was always the same, over and over, which became a little wearing for those of us who worked in the salon. Gossip around the salon generally tended to be repetitive, but this was a little harder to take because we knew it weighed on Betina.

For better or worse, by Tuesday afternoon the gossip and theories had gone completely wild. Someone came up with the novel idea that maybe the Paramabets, Mr. Keshian, and August were NSA agents, and the bad guys had located them here and were trying to draw attention to them. This theory did, at least, raise some new questions for people to bat around, not least among them: what would NSA agents be looking for in Knockemstiff?

The discussion was finally put to rest when someone asked, "Do you really think anyone in the NSA could make tacos as well as the Paramabets?" No one thought that sounded plausible. And no one asked how people from Delhi could make tacos that good. For people who grew up in Knockemstiff, it just made sense.

The next theory was space aliens. This idea was proposed in all seriousness by a fishwife who lived out by the bayou. "We see funny things out there," she said. Given the amount of cheap gin that was consumed along the bayou, this revelation came as no surprise.

The aliens may or may not have abducted the fishwife and experimented on her, but they certainly lifted the mood of people in the salon, aside from one or two who worried that the aliens might abduct and experiment on them. I suppose aliens are out there in the universe somewhere, and it's easy to believe that they are hundreds of times smarter than us on earth. Let's face it, human beings don't seem all that smart some days.

In any case, I've never been able to think of any earthly reason (or unearthly reason) why aliens could possibly be interested in me. I'm just not that interesting. If I were more interesting, maybe I'd have a steady boyfriend.

I thought about being interesting and having a steady boyfriend, mostly the latter, as I locked up the salon for the day and walked over to the Bacon Up Diner. Most Tuesday evenings I join friends at the Bacon Up for dinner, conversation, and a beer. If I felt extravagant, I'd have a glass of wine. Tonight was definitely a beer night.

As its name suggests, the Bacon Up specializes in putting bacon on or in nearly anything you can eat, if you can call that specializing. Try the bacon gumbo, hushpuppies with bacon bits, bacon beignets, or bacon-n-grits. Claude, the owner, said, frequently, "Bacon never hurt nothin'." Some of us thought to ourselves "except one's arteries."

Honestly, though, I don't worry too much about that sort of thing, which is probably why I'm not quite svelte. Technically, I average about a pound overweight, maybe two pounds after dinner at the Bacon Up. As my mama used to say, unknowingly quoting Oscar Wilde, "Everything in moderation, including moderation." I would add, "especially at the Bacon Up."

It's interesting to note that back when scientific research proved that the road to heart disease was paved with saturated fat, the news did not seem to decrease business at the Bacon Up. Nor did the Bacon Up see more business when scientific research eventually proved that saturated fat isn't much worse for you than unsaturated veggie oil.

It wasn't that the people of Knockemstiff are unimpressed by science. People here are largely admirers of the scientific method, just as they might admire a Massey Ferguson model 35 tractor that's still running or a person who can reliably tell a good joke.

No, the lack of a response to saturated fat was not due to a disrespect for science. It had more to do with the slow pace of life here. The decade or two after the onset of the saturated fat scare was simply not sufficient for people to come to terms with a new diet. By the time they had started to figure out what items in their diet to eliminate and what items to add and how to add those items, the whole thing was over, whoosh. As far as people in Knockemstiff were concerned, they might as well have been trying to catch a bullet in their teeth. Sorry, I do tend to get carried away with my own brand of banter.

On this particular Tuesday night, I decided to catch one of Claude's homemade boudin sausages in my teeth with a side of collards-n-bacon. Also the hushpuppies.

Although my friends found the theories about NSA agents and space aliens entertaining if unconvincing, nobody had anything better to offer. The general consensus was that some teenager was bored and decided to mix things up a bit. The whole matter would probably fade away in a week or two. August would convince her mother that she was not a slut. Life would return to normal.

For now, the events of the week had been a little trying, so it was a two-beer night for me. Two is about my limit — enough to make me glad I was walking home rather than driving.

I do weave just a little when I walk on two beers. Yes, I'm a lightweight.

I was one of the last to leave the Bacon Up, weaving goodbye. Knockemstiff has only one street light, which is in front of the post office, so I carried a flashlight in my purse. I don't use it when I walk familiar streets on a clear night, though. When my eyes adjust to the dark, I can see better by moonlight or just starlight. I get a better sense of what's around me. My daddy taught me that.

The heat of the day had ebbed by now. The usual afternoon showers had held off until evening. While I'd been in the diner, we'd had a couple of little thunder boomers that had rattled the windows but dumped most of their rain elsewhere. The sky had cleared, it was a pleasant evening, and I walked along the tree-lined street toward home thinking about something other than smashed and painted windows.

News I'd heard over dinner weaved through my thoughts. Jimmy and Lucile Pageant's daughter was expecting a boy. Lucile was making a quilt. The Emersons were adding a room onto their house.

As I turned onto Tennessee Street, my thoughts turned to home. My garden had been neglected lately, so if the showers held off over the weekend, I needed to do some serious weeding. I'd have some good tomatoes by now, along with the snap beans and okra. The crowder peas might not be producing much. The summer squash were already promising to bear multitudes.

Thinking about produce, I decided to invite Connor O'Sullivan to dinner. I'm not much of a Cajun cook, but he liked what I made or did a very convincing job of pretending to like it. I wondered if I was interesting enough to interest Connor. He created his own conversational whirl that carried me along. I always wondered if this effortless Irish *craic*, as he called it, indicated that he particularly enjoyed my company or he was just like that with everyone. Some people can't help but be interesting.

One positive point about my prospects with Connor was that when work took him out of town, he trusted me to take care of his dog, an old blue tick hound named Finnegan. This was an honest tribute on the part of any man in Louisiana.

I was 50 yards from my house on Tennessee Street, thinking about the dinner with Connor, when I saw the shape of a person lying on the grassy verge by the side of the road. The form was small, and I thought about Sarah sleeping on the lawn, but this person was bigger than that. And they were twisted in an unnatural way.

I rushed over and knelt down, took the person's shoulders in my hands and almost shouted, "Are you all right?" But I knew immediately that this person was not alright, not alright at all.

I fumbled in my purse for my flashlight, and it seemed like forever before I finally felt the familiar shape. When I switched on the light, I could see it was Annie Simmerson in her charcoal blazer. I could also see the blood, and I immediately stood upright with a pang of fear, shining the flashlight around me.

Annie was pretty clearly dead. Whoever or whatever had killed her might still be around. And if she wasn't dead she needed help that I couldn't give. I ran the rest of the way home and called the police, woke somebody up, who woke up our old police chief Tanner, who woke up the parish sheriff and lots of other people, who all arrived eventually at my little clapboard house and the grassy verge where Annie lay dead.

Chapter 4

When terrible things happen to me or around me, I get alarmed and then quickly settle into a steely calm. Well, settle is not the right word, because I feel like I'm watching events from somewhere high above everything. I've always found this experience remarkable and mysterious in retrospect. I seem to remember the sights and sounds of everything that happened, without remembering anything about how I felt at the time.

The rest of the night consisted of flashing lights, voices on police radios, questions from chief Tanner, and questions from a man in a rumpled sport coat who mumbled his name. After hours of lights and voices and little procedural details, I fell into bed and instantly passed from steely calm to dreamless sleep.

When the radio alarm went off two hours later, I opened my eyes in the early morning light to find myself fully dressed right down to my slightly muddy shoes. The steely calm was gone, and like a punch in the gut I recalled what I'd overheard the night before. One of the sheriff's deputies was crouched in the grass by Annie with bright lights shining from several directions. He looked up at the man in the rumpled sport coat and said, "Looks like maybe a thirty-ought-six. From just a few feet away." The deputy had made another sound that was something like "Awghh," stood up, and walked quickly away.

So I knew that Annie had been shot, maybe by a .30-06, which was an easy guess because approximately everybody in Richwater Parish had one of these rifles. I had one myself, inherited from my daddy. I'd never had any use for it or any expectation that I might decide to go deer hunting. I hung onto it for emotional reasons, a steel and wood reminder of my father that I kept locked in a closet.

A hot shower woke me out of my daze a little. I stood under the water for a long time. As I was getting dressed, I decided to drive to the salon today rather than walk. My house is only four tenths of a mile from the salon, but I couldn't picture myself walking along Tennessee Street.

In fact, I wasn't sure I wanted to be alone in my house on Tennessee Street after dark. That's how shook up I was -- I've never been afraid of living alone before. My parents raised me to be self-reliant, expected me to be capable of taking care of whatever needed doing, and I guess their expectations stuck.

It helped that Knockemstiff had always been a quiet, safe, charmingly boring little town. Now it didn't seem any of those things. By the time I was getting in my little Ford Escort for the drive to the salon, I'd decided to ask Betina if she'd come stay for a few nights. She had stayed with me once before after a hurricane knocked out power to the tiny little cottage her parents had set her up in before they left for Alaska.

A solid line of traffic was inching its way along Tennessee Street toward "downtown." Somebody politely let me into the line of cars and pickup trucks, and I could see the yellow police tape along the side of the road. They had put out sawhorses to block traffic from that side of the street. An officer was allowing traffic in one direction to pass around the sawhorses and then traffic in the other direction.

I waited my turn. Walking would have been faster. Rush hour in Knockemstiff usually consisted of a couple of dozen pickups and several minivans crossing through town at about the same time. Today, half the people in town wanted to see the crime scene.

As I rolled past the scene, keeping my eyes straight ahead, the officer directing traffic motioned for me to stop. I saw it was Digby Hayes, a friend of my parents and a member of the tiny under worked Knockemstiff police force since before I was born. He walked over, and I rolled down my window.

"Morning, Savannah," he said, touching his hat.

"Morning, Digby," I said.

He inclined his head toward the side of the road. "Sorry you had to see that," he said. "Hope you're OK."

"Yeah. Thanks. Tired."

He patted my shoulder. "You take it easy. And be careful, you hear?"

"Yep. I'll ask somebody to stay at my place for a while."

He squeezed my shoulder and stepped back, waving traffic on again.

The cars ahead of me were still inching their way past the yellow police tape draped over the sawhorses. I turned on the radio and pressed one station button after the other, looking for a decent song. Nothing sounded good. By the time I got to the last button, I was past the yellow tape.

At the front door of the salon, I went to put my key in the lock and found that the door was already open. Nellie, Betina and Pete were there ahead of me. They are never there ahead of me.

When I came in, they were sitting in the café area. They stopped talking and looked at me. After a couple of seconds, Nellie jumped up. Betina and Pete stood up too. Nellie said, "I made coffee, Savannah. Come have a cup."

Pete said, "We heard you didn't sleep so good last night. I picked up some leftover beignets from Claude at the Bacon Up." He held out a white cardboard carton.

I took a beignet and sat down.

Nellie handed me a cup of coffee. "Why don't you take the day off, Savannah? We can handle everything."

It hadn't even occurred to me to stay home. By myself. "I'm in a mood to cut some hair," I said.

None of them so much as raised an eyebrow.

"Did you get any sleep at all?" Betina asked.

I told them about how I'd woken up twisted in the sheets still wearing my clothes. "There's something about sleeping with your shoes on that's not restful," I observed. "It will have to do."

The day started slowly, even though the salon was full of people by 10:00 am. Nellie had brought in several folding chairs for the extra people she knew would show up.

Gossip in the salon was like a hot air balloon that went up with a little heat from *this* and a little heat from *that*. An actual tragedy this close to home punctured the balloon.

People murmured to one another quietly. The phrase most often heard across the room was "Poor Annie." We would all nod, and the room would be quiet for a while. Even Dolores Pettigrew was reduced to repeating "Poor Annie" and "I can't believe it," separated by long dramatic pauses.

I didn't say anything in particular. I cut hair and juggled the facts in my mind every way I could think of. Could the spray painting, broken windows and Annie's death be related? Surely they were related, but how?

I continued clipping with my scissors. At some point I noticed that I'd been cutting the hair on the left side of Margaret Simpson's head for a very long time. I stopped and looked up. Margaret was staring at me in the mirror with an expression that managed to mix concern with amusement. She said, "I was thinking about wearing my hair a little shorter for summer."

"You probably want *both* sides a little shorter then," I said, moving around to her right side. I rolled my eyes at myself. "This cut's on me."

"Seems like if you cut twice as much as usual I should owe you double," she said.

I stepped around to her left side and surveyed the cut as it stood so far. "I could stop there, and you would just owe the regular amount."

She turned her head from side to side, looking into the mirror. "I could do a comb-over."

"Or I could even it up and give you a fleet rate on the whole thing. How about that?" I proposed.

"Go for it," she said. "I'll wake you up when you've cut enough off the right side."

The murmuring continued in the salon, with "Poor Annie" rising up and falling back again like a wave. Eventually, a distressed woman in Betina's chair trying to put a good face on events said loudly, "It was just a terrible accident. People have accidents with guns all the time." Several people recalled hunting accidents. Pete said that his father had accidentally shot his mother in the thigh while cleaning his gun, thinking that the gun was not loaded. ("I'm pretty sure it was an accident," he said quietly to the woman in his chair.) Someone quoted the wisdom "There's nothing more dangerous than an unloaded gun." People were chiming in with observations about being careful with guns.

"It wasn't an accident," I said.

The salon went quiet.

"What?" said Nellie.

"It wasn't an accident," I repeated. This was news that everyone knew, and no one had wanted to say.

"Did the sheriff say that?" asked Nellie.

"She was shot from a few feet away. I heard a sheriff's deputy say that. Nobody was cleaning his "unloaded" gun in the dark by the side of the road when Annie happened to walk by. Nobody accidentally aimed a rifle at Annie's heart and accidentally pulled the trigger and accidentally walked away without telling anyone about it. That just doesn't make sense."

If the salon had been quiet before, it was now quieter than it had ever been, as quiet as a room can be when it's full of people whose hearts are racing. Everyone realized they were holding their breath at the same time and exhaled with a gasp. The room erupted into animated chatter.

"A murder in our quiet little town?"

"Surely not!"

"I can't believe it."

"Who would do such a thing?"

"Why would anyone hurt Annie, when everyone loves her?"

Then the speculation began. Nellie's contribution was, "It's probably that creepy old guy with no teeth who lives in the cabin at the swampy end of the bayou."

Dolores Pettigrew said, "I saw him in town just the other day, walking along with a gunny sack. That's suspicious, isn't it?"

"It could be if he hadn't been carrying that gunny sack everywhere he's gone for the past decade or two," said Pete.

But Dolores had moved on with her speculation. "You know, people often do these things for money. Do you think the Grosri owed Annie money?"

Other people named possible culprits. Reasons were given, mostly based on bad character. The more people offered ideas, the more clear it became that nobody knew anything.

At the Teasen and Pleasen Salon, we generally work through lunchtime, and then take a break at 1:30. On slow days, we've been known to take most of the afternoon off for siesta. This was not a slow day. I was looking forward to whatever part of an hour we could get. Nellie and Pete managed to shoo everyone out of the café area by 1:45.

When Nellie, Pete and Betina got their brown-bag lunches out of the back room I remembered that I had forgotten to bring a lunch. "I'm going to dash down to the Grosri and pick up a sandwich," I said.

"Ham and cheese?" Pete asked, holding out a sandwich. "I got it on my second run to the Grosri for pastries this morning." He had noticed I hadn't brought lunch.

"Pete, you're a dear." I kissed him on the cheek.

"Aw, shucks," he said. He handed me the sandwich and an RC Cola.

We all sat down in the café area.

"My brain isn't at the top of its game today," I said. "I keep thinking that all the events we've been seeing are related, but I can't think how that could be."

"Got me swinging," said Nellie. "You think the same person who painted and smashed windows killed Annie?"

"Maybe."

"How else could they be related?"

"What if the murderer hadn't actually intended to kill Annie?" asked Betina. "Like everybody's been saying, who would want to kill Annie? What if there's a predator on the loose? He bumped into Annie, tried to assault her, she resisted, and he shot her?"

"It could have been more or less random," mused Nellie.

"Except that he's preying on women!" said Betina. "Savannah, he could be in your neighborhood, on your street."

"Now, Betina," I said. "We don't know anything like that."

"But Savannah, just to be safe, why don't you come stay with me for a while?"

"Well, actually, I was going to…" *invite you to come stay at my place*, I was going to say. How thoughtless would that be? I managed to finish with something else: "…just barricade the doors and 'shelter in place,' as the disaster people call it."

"Savannah, really?" said Betina.

"You're welcome to stay with us," said Nellie. "But I can't guarantee your safety at my house. Or that you'd get any sleep."

I was shaking my head as Pete added, "You would also be welcome to stay at my place if the Widdah Jenkins would allow." The Widdah Jenkins was what everyone called Dafny Jenkins since her basset hound Buster had died, leaving her feeling alone in the big house she'd inherited from her grandfather. She rented rooms to a couple of young men and strictly forbade visitors, since it startled her to see anyone she wasn't used to having in the house.

I stopped shaking my head. "Thank you for your concern. I'll be fine." I took a long pull at my soda and swallowed. "Maybe I can get Connor to look in on me from time to time."

That plan met with general acclaim. They all knew that I liked Connor and would like to be able to like him better. Betina in particular had long been of the opinion that Connor O'Sullivan was a catch that just needed a bit of reeling in – an interesting opinion from a girl who played hard to get. I had no doubt that when she finally located exactly the man she was looking for, she would reel him in without delay.

Chapter 5

The rest of the afternoon passed in a whirl of speculation. By 4:00 pm I was out on my feet. My three salon cohorts finally prevailed on me to give it up. Nellie referred to possible "permanent damage" I'd inflicted on Lucille Braxton's A-line bob. Perhaps I would want to avoid further carnage? "Go home," she told me. "Now."

I didn't care to pass by the crime scene again, so I decided to walk home by a route that took me around the area. That would let me come up Tennessee Street toward home from the opposite direction.

This route took me past Annie's house, where I saw chief Tanner in the driveway talking with the man in the rumpled sport coat who had asked me questions the night before. The man was clearly a police detective. I wished I'd been able to understand him when he'd told me his name. James something?

Sheriff's deputies were carrying clear plastic bags out of the house. I could see that some of the bags contained spray cans. One bag contained clothes that obviously had red paint sprayed on them. Yet another bag contained half a dozen gold-colored objects that puzzled me until I realized what they must be: brass paperweights.

The deputies dumped the bags in the back of a police car. One of them said, "All done," to Tanner and the detective. When they looked around, they saw me standing in the street, staring with my mouth hanging open like a hick who'd never seen a driveway before. Tanner smiled and waved in a way that said "Wait a minute." He said one more thing to the detective, who nodded and stood eyeing me suspiciously.

Tanner walked over to where I was standing. "You headed home? Let me give you a lift."

"Thank you, Tanner. That's awfully nice of you," I said. It was while we were walking toward his ancient police car that I remembered I'd driven to the salon that morning. I stopped in mid-stride. "Uh, Tanner."

He turned and looked my way with his hand on the car door handle.

"I just remembered I drove to work this morning. I need to go back and get my car." I motioned back toward the salon and started to turn around.

He laughed. "Hop in," he said. "I'll drop you off at the salon."

As I sighed and got in the car, I couldn't help looking over at the detective, whose suspicious look was now mingled with a rough guess that I was an idiot – possibly a dangerous idiot.

"You worked all day?" Tanner asked me.

I nodded. "A couple of my clients' heads will look unusually bare for a while, I'm afraid."

"This would have been a good day for me to come in for my crew cut," he observed.

"Tanner, Annie was the one who broke the windows and did the spray painting, wasn't she?"

"Looks that way," he said. "There's nothing in her house painted red, so she was painting something else."

We had arrived at my car. Before I got out of the police car, I told him about the painted letters on Mr. Keshian's window that Nellie and I had found. He already knew about the painting of the Paramabets' window.

"I've never seen anything like it," he said. "It's all for the parish investigator to sort out, not me."

"The guy in the sport coat?" I asked.

"That's him. Investigator James Woodley."

"Does he seem like a man who's going to be able to sort this out?"

"He seems like a man who doesn't care if anybody thinks he's able to sort this out. He seems like a man who would rather be back in the Big Easy listening to jazz and drinking rum cocktails." Tanner gave me a wry smile. "So maybe he's a man who'll solve this boring little swamp-town case in a hurry so he can get outta here."

I got out of the car and thanked him.

"Digby said you've got somebody to stay with you for a while there on Tennessee Street?" Tanner asked.

"Yeah, well, I think my company might not arrive right away. I'll be alright."

"Mmm. Digby will be around there a lot, and the deputies are coming and going. Just be careful, OK? And get some rest."

"Will do."

I made an even bigger circle around town so I could avoid both the crime scene and Annie's house on my way home. I didn't want to risk seeing Investigator James Woodley again. Or having him see me.

Back at home, I made sure all the doors and windows were locked. I was tempted to fall into bed fully clothed again, minus shoes this time, but I made myself take a shower to wash off the hair clippings that seem to go everywhere.

I had a few bites of some microwaved Italian thing and settled thankfully into bed long before dark. And lay there awake. And lay there.

Figures. You get perfectly exhausted, and the last thing you can do is sleep.

I got a beer and some peach yogurt out of the fridge and plopped in front of the TV.

The next thing I knew somebody was screaming. Somebody else was shouting my name. There was a struggle.

I found myself staring up into Nellie's face. It turned out that she was the somebody shouting my name. To quote her precisely: "Savannah, you dimwit, it's me."

She found the remote and turned off the TV. I got a glimpse of Godzilla smashing buildings before the TV went dark, which plunged the room into complete darkness. Nellie turned the TV back on so she could find a light, and the smashing and screaming resumed.

Eventually, the table lamp was on, the TV off again, and Nellie stood in front of me. I was so confused, I looked at her like an idiot. I was getting good at that.

"Did you unplug your phone?" she demanded.

I admitted that I had.

"What if someone had called to warn you of something?"

"Maybe to warn me that you were coming to scare the wits out of me?"

"Good example. I tried to call several times over the course of an hour and finally figured you must be unplugged or dead."

"I didn't want any well-meaning concerned people calling and waking me up."

"Even if that meant a murderer could sneak up on you?"

"Well, if he killed me without waking me up, that would be OK."

"That's not funny," Nellie said.

"I didn't actually mean it to be funny," I said, shifting uncomfortably in my easy chair.

"You can't help being funny, can you?"

"I *feel* funny, now that you raise the topic," I said. I'd spilled half the peach yogurt in my lap. Luckily, we hadn't knocked over the beer in our little scuffle. I handed it to Nellie.

"What are you doing here?" I asked, trying to stand up at an angle that would keep the yogurt from running off my PJs.

"It was Rudy's idea," she explained.

"Rudy suggested that you come over and terrify me?" I asked over my shoulder as I slouched into the bathroom to shower off the yogurt – my third shower of the day.

"Right," she called around the corner. "He said, 'Since Savannah can't ask Betina to stay with her, why don't you go terrify her for a while? The boys and I will go camping over on the Tickfaw River.' That river has advantages over the swamp next to our house that include the presence of both alligators and crocodiles."

"So Rudy figured out that I was going to ask Betina to stay with me but couldn't on account of Betina was already terrified?"

"Right again," Nellie said. "You're smarter than you look, Savannah."

"I've been looking like a ditz lately." As I dried off and put on clean PJs, I told her about seeing Tanner and the detective at Annie's house and forgetting I had driven to work. "I'm sure that detective thinks I'm an idiot."

"Well, he came by the salon as I was locking up and wanted to talk to you. Maybe he enjoys idiotic chats."

"I'll bet Tanner told him what we found on Mr. Keshian's window when we went dumpster diving."

"Talk about idiotic things," Nellie reflected. "Anyway, I told him you had gone home to get some sleep, and could he come back tomorrow to talk to you. He said he would." She took a gulp of the beer and handed it to me. "Then Rudy decided I should come over here to make sure you sleep well."

"I was sleeping like a baby," I observed.

"Why were you watching that Godzilla movie?" she asked.

"I was exactly not watching that Godzilla movie," I said. "Did you not notice that my eyes were closed? Or did you assume I was watching my eyelids?"

"I noticed that I knocked on the door for a long time, and you didn't answer the door. I could hear the TV going, so I knew you were in here. When I finally used your spare key and found you sitting there unconscious, I thought I'd better wake you up to make sure you weren't dead."

"Thank you for coming," I said somewhat seriously.

"I'll thank Rudy for you," she said politely.

"Rudy decided they will stay safe in the swamp without you?"

"Yeah, at some point I figure I've got to let them take care of themselves. The oldest boy is more careful than his father. He can get them all out if they have a problem. Probably."

"Aubrey is 14?"

"He is 14, yes, and he can drive the truck and fix things and shoot an alligator, if necessary. Most importantly, he knows how to not shoot things."

"I'm sure they'll be fine," I lied cheerfully. "Let me make up the bed in the guest room for you."

"You go on back to sleep. I can find everything I need."

Chapter 6

I have heard that some people track their sleep with little electronic devices. Doesn't this tracking activity cut into the time they have for sleep?

My primary interest in sleep is sleeping. I find sleeping highly rewarding and do it every night if I possibly can.

I woke on Thursday morning to the sound of rain pouring down. I listened to it for a minute or two and fell asleep for another hour. This time when I woke up I could hear sizzling in the kitchen, and then my alarm went off.

Nellie was frying a big breakfast. "I saw what was left of what you ate last night and figured you needed to eat this morning," she said. She was right.

Over breakfast we talked about Annie's spray cans and paperweights.

"So is it logical to think that somebody killed Annie because she spray-painted and/or broke their window?" asked Nellie.

"It doesn't seem much of a motivation, does it," I said. "Even the SLUT thing is a thin reason to kill somebody." I chewed a bite of Jimmy Dean sausage. "Were you serious about the old guy on the bayou being the perp? The one with no teeth?"

"I kinda was. I wanted to put it out there to see if anybody else had anything to say about him."

"Dolores saw him the day Annie was killed?"

"That's what she said, yeah. She's suspicious of everybody, so ordinarily I wouldn't take her suspicions to mean much."

"Why are you suspicious then? Aren't you actually related to those people at the south end of the bayou?"

"Mmmm. I am. Thank you for remembering," she said. "I think of the old guy who lives alone in the shack as a very distant relation, but he's Rudy's grandfather."

"The toothless guy?"

"The toothless guy, *yes*." She looked at me with slight vexation. "If we're judging perp-worthiness based on oral hygiene, he's gotta be the most likely suspect."

"Sorry. I guess anybody can lose their teeth. I had no idea he was Rudy's grandfather. You suspect him, though?"

"I've been wary of him for a long time. He's just scary. One minute he's telling stories of working on barges along the Atchafalaya, talking about cheating at cards and fighting — boasting about fighting dirty. Then he's screaming about some guy who fired him and cutting the air with a wicked-looking knife. Even Rudy learned early on to keep out of knife range."

"If Annie had been killed with a knife, we'd know who to look for."

"The thing is, Dolores was right about him being in town that day, only she didn't notice that he had something bigger than usual in his gunny sack."

"As big as a rifle?" I asked.

"Just about," she said. "I only noticed because he was barging along in front of the hardware store with it and banged into Annie."

"Really? You mean, physically bumped into her?"

"Knocked that gunny sack into her leg as he went past. She said something to him, and it must have been a choice comment because he started yelling at her. I can't imagine what she said. He gets riled about things that happened in the past, but if anybody slights him nowadays, he says, 'Ohhhhhh,' in a singsongy way. Then he laughs and walks away. He wasn't laughing that day. And he wasn't walking away, but I don't think he pulled his knife. Annie walked away, and he didn't follow her. That was all I could see. I was driving by with the boys."

"Goodness. You think he's really capable of killing her?"

"I wouldn't call him harmless. He *is* Rudy's grandfather, though, so I'm not eager to sic the police on him."

"We could go talk to him, see if we can find out anything."

"Mmm, 'talk to him.' That makes it sound so simple." She stood up from the table and started clearing away the dishes. "We need to get you to the salon so you can talk to the in*spec*tor."

"Investigator."

"Whatever," she said.

"We might as well cut some hair so long as we're there."

* * *

The rain had slacked off to a moderate downpour, which didn't keep people from filling up the salon. The news that Annie had done the spray-painting and window smashing shocked everyone. Or almost everyone.

A woman that we didn't normally see in the salon came in around 11:00 am. Her hair was a little ragged, and her cotton dress wasn't much better. Nellie recognized her as the mother of a boy who sometimes played with her three sons and called out, "Hey Jewel." The woman bobbed her head and sat in the café area.

"Something going on there," Nellie whispered to me. "She lives on a dirt road out along the swamp that borders our house. I don't think I've exchanged a dozen words with her in all the years I've known her."

Jewel sat quietly in the café area and listened intently as everyone talked about the shocking news that Annie must have done the recent mischief in town.

"Did she not get along with the Paramabets?"

"Everybody gets along with them."

"Even if she didn't get along with them, why smash their window?"

"And Mr. Keshian's?"

"And what could she possibly have against August?"

"Even if she was jealous of August or something like that, why spray-paint her windshield? That's so childish."

"This vandalism just don't sound like anything Annie would do," said Pete. "It makes me wonder if someone is trying to set her up. Annie was a sweet soul who wouldn't harm anyone."

"That is not acc'rate," Jewel said quietly.

Nellie's head snapped around to face Jewel. Betina, who hadn't heard Jewel, was agreeing with Pete.

Nellie spoke over Betina, "What did you say, Jewel?"

"I said, that is not acc'rate." She was sitting with her fists clinched, looking down at the floor. "That is not right 'bout Annie bein' a sweet soul. She was a devil, that one."

The salon had gone quiet. Nellie put down her scissors and comb. She walked over to where Jewel was sitting and knelt down beside her.

"Tell me," she said.

Jewel closed her eyes. "When I went to Dr. Cason near about two year ago with the terrible pain in mah gut, Annie tole me after I saw the doctor that he had found a malignancy, and there weren't nothin' anybody could do about it. I was a-goin' to die."

Jewel opened her eyes and looked at Nellie. "That's what she said to me. 'Miz Laborde, you're gonna die. You might as well go home and make your peace.' That's what she said."

Nobody in the salon moved a muscle. I wondered if this was the most this reclusive woman had ever said in her life. Jewel looked down at the floor and wrung her hands.

"Franklin, my husband, was tore up about it," she said. "We tried to think how the family would get on when I was no longer there. It was hard to do." Jewel looked around at people in the room. "Whenever I did anything, I was always thinkin' *Who's a-goin' to do this when I'm gone?*"

She made a short gesture with her hand — time passing. "A few months went on. Mah pain got better, but I was all knotted up inside like a bramble. One day Franklin was in town and runned into Dr. Cason, and said couldn't he do something about my malignancy, *please*, and Dr. Cason was surprised, and said *What's this you say?*, and he related that he had found not a thing wrong with me but something bad I musta ate. He tole Franklin that I musta misunderstood what Annie said."

Jewel looked at Nellie, then looked around at all the people staring at her. "I did not misunderstand nothin'. That woman was bein' a devil. And I never done nothin' to her, *nothin'*. I went back to that doctor office and axed her why. She look at me and just smiled. 'That was just a mistake,' she says."

Jewel stood up. "You wonder why that woman smash winders and paint everything?" she said. "I come to tell you why. Pure meanness. She was a devil."

She walked out of the salon with Nellie right behind her.

For the second time in a week, the salon was completely quiet. When Nellie came back a few minutes later, she said she'd got Mrs. Ourso at the feed store to take her lunch break early and drive Jewel home.

What was left of the morning passed slowly. The people in the café area drifted out, shaking their heads. When 1:30 rolled around, the last remaining customer paid for her perm and left.

We sat down to eat our late lunch. Nellie unwrapped the sandwiches she'd made for us.

I looked at her. "So did Jewel kill Annie?"

"I asked her," Nellie said. "I hated to, but I had to. I didn't want to have that investigator go out there to plague her." Nellie put down her sandwich. "He'll plague her anyway." She shook her head. "When I asked her if she shot Annie, Jewel looked me in the eye and told me, 'I never did. That would make me a devil, too.'"

We ate our lunch wondering if there were two Annie's in our town.

* * *

By 3:00 pm the salon was once again full of people. Word of Jewel's story had gotten around town, and people came in to talk about it. None of us who had heard the story first hand were all that eager to talk about it. We let the newcomers who didn't know anything do all the talking.

While other people talked, I cut hair and thought about evil.

It was tempting to think that people did evil deeds because they were idiots, as little Sarah would say. In her world, anyone who did bad things just didn't understand the consequences, so they must be stupid.

My daddy taught me that people do things because they want something. It's just not always clear what they want.

I remember a November day when I was maybe 10. I was slopping the hogs toward the end of the day. I remember it was November because Thanksgiving was coming up soon. It was late enough in the year so that the weather was cool, and it had been spitting rain on and off all day.

We didn't live on a farm, but we had a few chickens and pigs. One of my chores was to feed the pigs. Some of them were cute little porkers that were born in the spring, but we had one big old sow that was scary. She could be aggressive. And all that grunting did not seem friendly.

Since I was a little afraid of the sow, and even the little pigs could get wild when food was in sight, Daddy had set up a feed trough in a fenced enclosure that kept the pigs out until I was ready for them. I'd dump a bushel of corn into the trough along with whatever table scraps Mama had sent out. Then I left the enclosure before reaching over the fence to unlatch the gate that let in the pigs. The latch was a metal rocker that was easy to hit with the heel of my hand.

All the pigs would be standing at the gate, watching my every move, grunting impatiently, ready to shove the gate open. The instant I banged the gate latch open, the stampede started, with the sow in the lead and the little porkers jostling behind her, squealing.

On this particular day, one of our dogs — a big black mutt named Collier — had gone into the enclosure with me and stayed in there when I left. I guess he was sniffing for table scraps, but Mama hadn't sent out anything a dog would want to eat. Collier could easily jump out of the enclosure, so I left him standing in the trough, sniffing. I walked around to the gate where the pigs were waiting and hit the latch.

The stampede went nowhere. The pigs stood outside the gate shuffling back and forth, looking at Collier and looking at me and looking back at Collier, who had stopped sniffing and stood looking at the pigs. I don't know why I didn't shoo Collier out of the trough. I was cold and wet and ready to go inside. I guess I was curious about what would happen.

Finally, the sow couldn't stand it anymore and shoved open the gate, but she still wasn't willing to get close to the trough. Collier barked at her, wagged his tail, sat down, barked again. He looked like he was enjoying himself rather a lot. He barked a couple more times. He looked over at me and raised his head with an expression indicating that he clearly was pleased with himself.

At that point, Daddy came around the corner of the house and saw Collier in the trough and the pigs slobbering and grunting by the gate. It suddenly dawned on me that I'd been standing there allowing Collier to keep the pigs from eating – poor pigs! It was like a whole new point of view had walked around the house and into my own head.

I thought Daddy would yell at Collier to get out of the feed trough, but he didn't say anything right away. He walked over to where I was standing and said, "What do you suppose Collier wants?"

"He wants to sit in the trough?" I said.

"Apparently. And what does he want to get by sitting in the trough?"

"Well, I've never seen a dog eat ears of corn," I thought out loud. "And there's no scraps a dog would want."

"So he doesn't want what's in the trough. Do you think he knows that the pigs want what's in the trough?"

"He looks like he does. So he wants to keep the pigs from eating?"

"Sure looks like he does." Daddy shifted into his falsetto school marm voice. "And what does he get from that?"

"He gets to sit there like king of the hill."

"Yep. Most people would say he's not getting anything out of having that trough. But *he* thinks he's in charge. Top dog." He turned to the dog. "Don't you feel good about that?"

Collier wagged his tail slightly, but something about Daddy's tone of voice was not convincing. Daddy motioned the dog to come away as he said in a low voice, "Get on down, you sorry mutt."

At Daddy's dismissive tone, the dog's ears drooped and he lowered his head. Daddy snapped his fingers, and Collier slunk out of the feed trough, hopped the fence, and trotted away.

As the pigs stampeded to their dinner, he and I walked back to the house for our dinner. "Some people are like that," he said. "They feel like they've got something great when they get to lord it over others."

"But why do they feel that way, Daddy?"

"Don't you like being in charge, my little princess?" He began a mincing walk like a princess with her nose in the air. I'd seen this before.

I swatted his arm.

"*Every*body wants to be in charge," he said in his school marm voice, which was now a princess voice. He stopped prancing, opened the back door of the house, and bowed me in like a royal page. "Nothing wrong with being a princess," he said, "but don't keep the pigs from the trough."

***

Did Annie really treat Jewel so badly? I was sure Jewel wasn't lying. And in hindsight, Annie's sweet nature looked too good to be true. But I still held out hope that Jewel had misunderstood. My mama always said to not speak ill of the dead.

It certainly looked as though Annie had been doing some bad mischief, however, and my daddy would say that she had some reason. If that were the case, what did Annie want?

Chapter 7

Investigator James Woodley finally arrived at the salon a little before closing time wearing the same rumpled sport coat I'd seen him in before. He looked like he's just woken up from a rough night. I motioned him toward our back room while I finished the haircut I was working on.

Nellie asked if he'd like a cup of coffee. "We don't usually drink coffee this late," she said, peering at his haggard face, "but you look like you could use a cup." He accepted the cup she handed him without comment and took it into the back room.

Some of the people in the salon looked puzzled at the presence of this quietly intense stranger. Those in the know filled them in. I was surprised that the investigator had managed to keep such a low profile in this small town. I guessed that this might have something to do with his not being seen much during daylight hours.

When I finished the haircut, I went into the back room. Woodley was sitting on a stack of cardboard boxes, sipping his coffee and reading notes he'd made on a tiny pad of paper he held cradled in his hand.

He stood up when I came in and closed the door behind me.

"Ms. Jefferies," he said, extending his hand toward a rolling desk chair, the only chair in the room, without really looking me in the eye.

"Investigator Woodley," I said. I sat down. "What can I help you with?"

"Chief Tanner tells me that you found spray painting on the window of Mr. Keshian, the owner of the shoe repair shop." He continued to look absently in the direction of his notes. "Is that correct?"

"Yes."

"Could you describe what you found, please?"

I told him about the red-painted shards of glass that Nellie and I had pulled out of the dumpster.

"What kind of paint would you say this was?" he asked.

"Spray paint, the same shade of red and the same type of letters as on the Paramabets' window."

He surprised me by looking up from his notes. He fixed me with his piercing gray eyes in a way that was disturbingly intense. "You saw the paint on the Paramabet window before it was broken?"

"Ah, no. No." His attention was making me feel clumsy, vaguely guilty. "I went by there for take-out food and saw where Connor O'Sullivan had reassembled the broken glass."

"Connor O'Sullivan?"

"The man who fixed the window."

"He had reassembled the broken pieces of the original window?"

Had he not seen that glass? Had Connor thrown it away?

"Yes, sir," I said. Where did that come from? "I mean, yes."

I told him what Connor had put together and what we thought the spray-painted word was. "Didn't you see it?"

Woodley didn't answer. He continued to look at me in a vaguely accusatory way.

Finally it dawned on me why he hadn't seen it. "You didn't see anything that happened before Annie was killed." And he couldn't admit that because it made him seem ignorant? This man needed help.

"Do you want to see the pieces of Mr. Keshian's window?" I asked him.

His eyes went a little wide before he got them under control.

"You know where the pieces of Mr. Keshian's window are?"

I got up and walked over to the end of the room where Nellie and I had stashed the painted shards of glass at the end of our dumpster-diving expedition. I pointed down at the space behind a small cabinet. "I know exactly where they are," I said.

He walked over and peered down at the glass. He looked back at me, took a handkerchief out of his pocket, used it to pick up one of the pieces, and held it to the light. "What are you doing with this?"

"I'm not doing anything with it." Did he think I wanted to make a broken-glass collage?

"Why do you have the broken, spray-painted pieces of another person's vandalized window, Ms. Jefferies?"

My mouth dropped open. I closed it as soon as I could. I thought of that time my daddy had appeared around the corner of the house and brought with him a whole new point of view, only this time I seemed to be the dog in the trough.

"Uh," I said.

"Were you involved with Annie Simmerson in vandalizing the window? Did you break it after she painted it?"

"No!" I said.

"Yet you get some kind of pleasure from collecting the pieces of glass?"

"Pleasure? No, of course not. This is ridiculous."

"Is it?"

"Yes. And," I reflected, "everyone says that, don't they?"

He looked down at his tiny pad of paper and wrote something on it. "I'll tell you someone who doesn't say that, Ms. Jefferies. Annie Simmerson doesn't say that. And she doesn't say that because she's been murdered." He looked back at me. "What I want to know is, what's your involvement in Annie Simmerson's death?"

"Look," I said, "I heard about August's window being painted, I saw the broken window at the Paramabets', and it made me wonder if Mr. Keshian's window had been painted before it was smashed. I had seen him cleaning up the glass because he's just a couple of doors down from here. I knew he'd put the glass in the dumpster out back. I didn't think the Knockemstiff police would follow up on it. I was just curious."

"Killed the cat, Ms. Jefferies," he said as he wrote something on his pad. "Killed the cat."

"Including the professionally curious cat, Mr. Woodley?"

He looked up. "Is that a threat, Ms. Jeffries?"

I was putting on my stupid look to follow my alarmed look when I noticed that Investigator Woodley was smiling. Just a little.

"You knew all along I had nothing to do with Annie," I said.

"Ah, well," he said looking back down at his notes. He took a gulp of coffee, which must have been cold by now. "It's not entirely true that you had nothing to do with Annie. Besides finding her dead, I mean."

"Certainly, I knew her. Lot's of people knew Annie."

"And you in particular knew her well enough to ask her to walk Sarah Jameson home on Monday morning."

"Yes," I said. "That was the morning after Mr. Keshian's window was broken."

"And did you know that Sarah arrived home crying?"

"Sarah's mother told me, yes. I assumed it was because Sarah was upset by the broken window. She and Annie walked right past it, and Annie spoke with Mr. Keshian."

"Sarah may have been upset by Mr. Keshian, but she was crying for another reason. Did you give her a lollipop?"

This man had done more legwork than I gave him credit for. "I did give her a lollipop. How do you know about the lollipop? Or I should ask, why is the lollipop important enough for you to want to know about?"

"Details, Ms. Jefferies. The devil is in them."

I thought of Jewel calling Annie a devil.

"In this case," he continued, "one detail is that Annie asked Sarah if she knew that lollipops make little girls stupid."

"Sarah is a smart little girl. That would bother her."

"If she believed it. Another detail is that Annie snatched the lollipop out of Sarah's mouth and tossed it in one of the lovely trash bins you people have put up in this town. That bothered Sarah a lot. And that's why she arrived home crying."

"Another bit of Annie meanness," I said. Then I remembered that the previous bit of meanness I'd heard was from Jewel, and I was hoping I could avoid mentioning that. I wanted to spare her an interrogation like this one. Was this obstructing justice? I thought that Woodley had plenty of evidence about Annie's meanness. And I was sure that Jewel was not a murderer. Fortunately, Woodley let my comment pass.

"And another detail," he said, "is that Sarah's father was upset when Sarah told him what Annie had done. Do you know Mr. Jameson?"

I thought of Sarah sleeping on the lawn with her daddy's rifle. "Not very well. Bee Jameson is a regular at the salon, but we don't see her husband Lester much. Surely you don't think he'd kill Annie over a lollipop?"

"Apparently, he had other reasons to be angry with Annie. You wouldn't happen to know anything about that?"

"News to me," I said. "But I'm finding out a lot about Annie that I didn't know. It's odd that in a town this small, Annie was so poorly understood."

"Mmm," he said. "Depends on who you ask."

"Could I ask you something, Investigator Woodley?"

"You can ask," he said. He said it in a way that implied that he asked questions; he did not answer questions.

"Could you tell me if Annie was sexually assaulted the night she was killed?"

"Yes, I can tell you that, no, she was not sexually assaulted. At least, we found no evidence of it. That's the kind of information we'd release to the press if there were any members of the press here. You seem to be living in this planet's only press-free bubble."

"We had a weekly newspaper when I was little," I said. "Now it's word of mouth."

"A game of post office then."

"Yes, for a small town it can become a rather large game of post office, with certain people passing on increasingly creative 'information' every time they have a conversation." I thought of an anthrax scare we'd had the year before. News of a farmer's test for anthrax was blown up into an imminent terrorist attack in which anthrax bombs were about to rain from the sky. Knockemstiff's little Botowski Hardware store sold out of plastic sheeting and duct tape in an hour and a half.

"Say," I offered, "what if we post official news releases from you on our bulletin board? It would be like having a little newspaper."

"Good idea. People could come in to find out what's going on. That would help your business, wouldn't it?"

Just when I was starting to think he was a decent human being, he says this.

"Possibly," I said. "Let me check."

I went out to the salon and looked around quickly. Everyone stopped what they were doing and stared at me. I popped back into the back room.

"One of the extra folding chairs we put out in our café area is currently unoccupied, so you're right, Investigator Woodley. Posting official news about the case could increase our business. If we could suck in one more person, that would be highly profitable for us — another couple of dollars in the collection basket for pastries. And coffee."

I picked up his half-full cup of cold coffee and poured it in the sink.

"Any other questions I can answer for you, Investigator Woodley?"

"Sorry, Ms. Jefferies." He stood and bowed his head in a gracious apology. "I accused you groundlessly."

"That seems to be your stock in trade," I observed, not quite ready to let him off the hook.

"And it is effective. You'd be surprised how often it turns a practiced song and dance into a confession. You can learn a lot by putting people under a little bit of pressure."

"I suppose."

"Please do understand that it's nothing personal. A woman has been murdered. That's intolerable. She might not have been the Susie Sunshine that some people thought, but she didn't deserve to be murdered. I have to find the murderer, whatever it takes."

Maybe he was a decent person after all.

He was looking at his tiny pad. "A couple more things that might help. Do you happen to know Annie's family?"

"I remember she had an older sister who lived here for a while. I can't recall ever meeting her parents. Odd."

"Have you met everyone else's parents?"

"You jest, but yes, I have, just about. And if I haven't met someone's parents, I know some reason why. With Annie, there's just a blank. Sorry. I'm surprised you didn't find that info on her phone."

"Phone?" he said with some excitement. "Annie had a cell phone?"

"I saw her with one. Just once. I suppose she could have borrowed it?"

The electricity went out of his excitement. "Yeah. One last question, please: the night that Annie was shot, did you hear that shot?"

"No! I hadn't thought about that. How could that be? A thirty-ought-six makes a lot of noise."

"How did you know it was a thirty-ought-six?" he asked, his suspicion getting a reprise.

"I heard a deputy say so, and he also said that it was from a few feet away, and that's how I knew that Annie had been murdered."

"Right. Thanks. There were thunderstorms in the hours before you found the body. Still, someone should have heard the shot. It wouldn't have sounded like thunder."

"Everybody in town knows what a thirty-ought-six sounds like," I said.

"Is that because everybody in town has one?" he asked ruefully.

"Just about," I said. "I ran into a six-year-old recently who was carrying one. I suppose that would make her a suspect."

"If this was the six-year-old I'm thinking of, she definitely had a motive, but she also had a strong alibi."

We walked out of the back room. Everyone was staring again.

Betina came over and said, "I took care of your 4:30. Is your interrogation over?"

"Interview!" Woodley said.

"If it's over," Betina said to me, looking at Woodley and ignoring him at the same time, "some of us are going to the Bacon Up before the open mic starts."

"Good plan," I said. "Don't want to do open mic on an empty stomach."

I was raised to include people in whatever was going on, so before I could stop myself, I invited Woodley to go with us to the amateur night goings-on at the Knockemback Tavern. It was one of those invitations like when people are visiting the house near supper time and you say, "Y'all stay for supper," without ever intending they should stay for supper, and they don't.

I was relieved when Woodley declined my invite, and then heard myself say, "Open mic would be good for your research, Inspector Woodley. You'd get to meet people who live here."

"Investigator," he said. "And maybe you're right. Thank you for inviting me."

Well great, I thought. Open mic night was going to be subdued after the murder. Now I'd gone and shot a tranquilizer dart in its posterior.

"Great," I said out loud. "Let's get us some bacon." Half a dozen of us headed for the diner.

Chapter 8

Dinner at the Bacon Up was indeed a restrained affair for the first 20 minutes or so. Nobody knew what to do with Woodley, me least of all, and nobody could have a conversation that didn't include him. So everything revolved around Woodley, except nothing was revolving. What do you say to a detective who's investigating a murder in your little town?

"So how's the murder thing going?" It was one of those rare times when the conversation could have been improved by Dolores Pettigrew, who would have chattered away about whatever random factoids passed through her head.

Then Nellie said something about a bar in Baton Rouge that Woodley had visited. This turned out to be a rich vein of conversation, relatively speaking, because Woodley had visited a lot of bars. He was busy replying to whatever Nellie had said when Margie, the waitress, started bringing food.

"That's the shrimp-and-grits for you, hon" she said, putting down the plate in front of me. "And the fried chicken for your date?"

Woodley's head whirled around as if he'd been whacked with a tennis racket. Before he could open his mouth, I said to him, "You wish!"

The poor man was stuck in a jam with his mouth open. I felt so sorry for him. Not.

Margie interrupted his thoughts. "You want this fried chicken or not?" As she set the plate in front of him, she winked at me. If you need help managing somebody, ask a waitress.

After that, Woodley made a point of chatting up the people on the side away from me, which livened up that half of the table and left me free to turn away from Woodley and talk with Betina. We talked about a little of *this* and a little of *that* in a way that made me think Betina had something on her mind.

She mentioned that she was concerned about the elaborate wrought-iron rack the salon had "inherited" when Mrs. Houghnard had closed her shop next door and gone to live with her sister in Atlanta. Everyone had called her Madame Houghnard. She ran her shop for 43 years, a little longer than I've been on earth. She carried whatever she thought was elegant and that people in Knockemstiff would buy — not a combination you'd think would work. With a few antiques, fancy stationary, even unusual baked goods, she made it work. Everyone in town missed her, and the salon had become custodian of the fancy display rack that was a reminder of the woman we no longer got to see. Betina told me that one of the legs had broken, so I made a mental note to ask

Connor O'Sullivan if he could fix it.

We talked about the young man Betina had gone out with the previous weekend. That seemed so long ago now.

Finally, Betina mentioned what was really on her mind: August. Betina had had no contact with August since the phone conversation on Monday that was just after the SLUT painting was found on August's windshield.

"I call her and go by her duplex every day," she said. "Since Tuesday, her car has not been in the driveway."

"Have you talked to the Bald Eagle since Monday? Maybe he's seen her come and go from next door."

"If I can't locate August over the weekend, I'll ask him when he comes for his haircut on Monday."

We knew from other people that August had not worked at the Grosri all week. August's disappearance was troubling as well as suspicious.

"I hate to ask," I said, "but she doesn't own a rifle, does she?"

Betina made a face. "She might. When she was in high school, she used to go deer hunting with her uncle. I *tried* to get her to join me for boy-related activities. She'd rather spend time in the woods with her uncle and a bunch of dogs." Betina rolled her eyes. "Just thinking of the ticks, uhh."

I didn't want to wonder out loud if August could possibly be capable of shooting Annie. Instead I said, "I wonder if *he's* looking for August." I gestured with my head in Woodley's direction.

"I wonder if he knows where she is," Betina said.

"If he does, he's not likely to tell you."

With a look of mock surprise, Betina said, "Why Savannah, whatever makes you think that he wouldn't tell me anything I want to know?"

"Betina, dear, good luck to you with that one."

***

The Knockemback Tavern was not crowded. We divided up around three tables facing the little "stage" area at one end of the room, where a stool and a microphone were waiting for whoever was brave enough to perform. In truth, it didn't take a great deal of bravery. This was an easy audience.

I made sure I sat at a different table from Woodley. I was impressed with how reluctant Betina looked in taking a seat at his table – step one of her research effort.

Open mic night was a long-standing tradition in Knockemstiff. I guess that goes without saying, since nearly everything that happened in Knockemstiff was a long-standing tradition.

The format was that each performer paid $2 and got 7 minutes at the mic. At the end of all the performances, whoever was still in the tavern got to vote on the best act of the evening. The winner got $20. The "rule" was that the winner had to spend the money at some business in town in the next week. Nobody enforced the rule, and winners usually thought it was part of the fun to blow the money right away.

The first act consisted of three sisters, aged 12, 14 and 15, who sang a boy band tune about being unwilling for life to go on for anyone if they couldn't be together. This choice was unfortunate in light of the murder that had just occurred, and I started to think it might be a long evening.

Next was a rapper, followed by a middle-aged guy with an accordion who sang a zydeco tune. He seemed to be singing a different song from the one he was playing on the accordion. That might be the way zydeco is supposed to sound. I don't really know.

Then we had something new: the Bald Eagle had decided to try his hand at stand-up comedy. We all clapped and cheered for him and got ready to groan.

"Knockemstiff is pretty backward," he began. He turned his head expectantly and waited. "I said, Knockemstiff is pretty backward." This time he put his hand to his ear.

"How backward is it?" someone finally asked.

"Knockemstiff is so backward," the Eagle said, "When airline pilots fly over the town, they don't even bother looking at their instruments because they know they won't be working."

We were so confused by this that we couldn't pretend to laugh, even though we were willing to pretend to laugh.

"See, the place is so backward, it's like back in time so stuff doesn't work?" A couple of people laughed at the idea that this was supposed to be funny. The rest of us groaned. The Eagle moved on.

"OK! Knockemstiff is so backward, we've never had decent cell phone coverage. We've heard about 3G or 4G technology, but forget that. People with cell phones in Knockemstiff are happy when they can say, "Gee, I got a connection!"

The audience rewarded him with a chorus of groans for that one. I applauded with the others and thought about the cell phone I'd seen Annie using. Where could it be?

The next performer was Sarah's mother, Bee Jameson, in the red dress that Sarah had told me about, the one that had prompted Bee's husband to wonder where she might be going in it. I'd been about as sure as he was that Bee was going someplace special in that dress, so it was nice to see that the special place was the open mic. Bee sang a couple of Broadway songs to music that she played from a boom box. The red dress was definitely the best thing about her act.

A couple of performers later we had a rare treat: a performer who was actually good. This was a 19-year-old named Leander, the son of former sharecroppers who now had their own farm near Knockemstiff. We saw him now and then at open mic.

He started the way he always did. He sat down on the stool, started playing his incredibly beat up 12-string guitar, and said, "Delta blues," as he played. Then he sang in a deep bass voice and stomped his feet from time to time. I think he was singing "rollin' and tumblin'" but I don't know anything about the blues. I really enjoyed his performances, though, so maybe I like the blues.

When Leander transitioned out of his first song straight into a second one about being a voodoo child, I heard Woodley bark a laugh. He was leaning forward slightly, listening enthusiastically to the music. I didn't know why he'd laughed. What's funny about a voodoo child? But it seemed to be an appreciative laugh. Leander glanced in Woodley's direction with the slightest trace of a twinkle in his eye.

When the song was over, everyone applauded. Woodley jumped to his feet clapping his hands. This was not common practice at open mic, but we all took the cue and gave Leander a standing ovation. This was fun. Why had we never done this before? Somebody yelled "Encore!" We all repeated the call – another new experience for open mic.

Leander was accepting the applause without seeming particularly moved by it. "Thank y'all," he said. He started playing again. "Here's a classic delta blues that I just wrote." He sang a rollicking blues number that everyone was enjoying until he got through the chorus:

Payday would be the first day of the week

We'd all have cars that were long and sleek

Women would wear the most beautiful jewels

If I was making up the rules

Every dog would have a musical bark

Nobody would ever get shot in the dark

I would never feel like a terrible fool

But I'm not making up the rules

We clapped uncertainly at the end of it. Woodley got up immediately and spoke to Leander. Could Woodley be "interviewing" Leander about the murder just because of the song?

Leander looked surprised. He turned back to the microphone and said, "Sorry, y'all, I didn't know. Them's the blues."

Woodley said something else to Leander and handed him his card. The mic picked up what Woodley said this time, "Give me a call. I know a bar owner in New Orleans who'll pay you to sing in a heartbeat."

We had a several other people who sang and played guitar, none as good as Leander. Connor O'Sullivan also read one of his poems, as he did every week. He usually *performed* a poem rather than just read it, but this week he was a little subdued. I remembered how upset he was when he was working on the Paramabets' window. He must still be upset. I suppose poets are like that, even if they're also blacksmiths.

"Pace off for me two yards of land," he read. "I'll plow it and plant, and get by as best I can, even alone and so far from home as I am."

OK, that actually went beyond subdued all the way to homesick. Before Connor left, I made an appointment with him to come look at the rack in the salon.

Leander won the $20.

Chapter 9

Nellie continued to stay at my house. "I might as well vacation at your house until my boys come home," she said, as we left the tavern. "If they come home."

"What I like about you, Nellie, is your unflagging optimism."

"And did you notice I used the term 'vacation' in there? Talk about optimism."

"As part of your vacation package, we include garden watering and weed whacking over the weekend."

"Wow," she said. "I feel like I'm at the Hilton."

The next morning dawned clear and bright. I walked out to my jungle and picked a couple of tomatoes that were perfectly ripe, picturing BLTs for lunch. I pulled a couple of major weeds, but it would take some dedicated work to make the jungle look like a garden again.

When I came back in the house with the tomatoes, Nellie was frying breakfast.

"You're handy to have around," I told her. "You can vacation here as long as you want."

She didn't look up. "As long as I want," she said. "What a concept."

She forked a couple of fat sausages onto plates for us and noticed the tomatoes I'd put on the counter. "What do you have there?"

"Vegetables from the jungle," I said.

"Fruit." She grabbed one of the tomatoes.

"Tomatoes are fruit?"

"That's the rumor." She quartered the tomato and plopped it into the frying pan.

"So we're having fried fruit for breakfast?"

"Grilled to-MAH-toes, as my English grandmother would say."

I'd never heard of Nellie having an English relation. "Where did this English grandmother come from?"

"England," she said. She pulled the toast out of the toaster.

"Could you be more specific?" I asked.

"Blackpool, England."

"There's a town called Blackpool?" I wondered. "But I mean, specifically, I never heard about you having an English anything in your background. I'm learning so much about your family lately."

"Yeah, my husband's grandfather is a swamp rat, and my grandmother Kirby was probably the English equivalent, although I might have jumped to that conclusion after hearing the name 'Blackpool.' Any town named that in Louisiana would be a swamp."

"*Any* town in Louisiana is a swamp," I said, sitting down at the table. "Never mind the name."

"Well, if we had one town that wasn't a swamp, we'd name it Parched, but that's what the English would name their swamp, if they had one. On the other hand, they'll name a nice little seaside resort town Blackpool and think it's sweet. Of course, I didn't know that when I was a kid."

She put the plates on the table. "You know how you grow up hearing stories that adults tell each other, and you can tell that you're not supposed to know what they're saying and shouldn't ask? Many of those stories in my family were about the Kirbys."

She sat down, and we started in on breakfast.

"I didn't know grandma Kirby very well," Nellie said, "but the two or three times we went to visit her over on the other side of Paudy, she fried tomatoes for breakfast. I thought that made a first-class breakfast."

"Mmm," I agreed. "That does go nicely with Claude's homemade sausage. You are handy indeed. As I say: vacation as long as you want."

She looked at me as she chewed. After a moment she asked, "Can I sit here and eat breakfast as long as I want?"

"So long as you want to eat for another," looking at my watch, "46 minutes."

She took another bite and chewed thoughtfully. "I'm trying to get my head around the as-long-as-I-want thing," she said.

"Maybe you need to think of vacation a little more broadly," I suggested, spreading my arms out to indicate what I meant by "broadly."

"Like broadly enough to include work, and weeding the garden, and other things that I don't want to do?"

"You don't want to work, really?" I asked.

"Sure, yes, of course. I like work, Savannah. Just not when I feel like sitting here eating breakfast," she explained. "For as long as I want."

"You could call in sick," I said.

"Another new concept!" she said. "You're winding me up this morning, Savannah. I can't remember if I've ever called in sick."

"You've stayed home when one of your boys was sick. Or all of them."

"That's calling in when somebody else is sick. I can't remember ever staying home because I was sick."

"I tell you what," I said standing up from the table. "Why don't you sit here for as long as you want." I got a portable phone off the kitchen counter and set it next to her plate. "Give me a few minutes to get to the salon and then call in sick."

"You're mean."

"I'm not trying to be mean. I'm serious. Take the day off."

"Savannah, there's no need to be so literal. I don't want to actually sit here all day. I want to feel like I could sit here all day if I wanted to, like if I was the richest woman on earth." She stood up and put the phone back. "Who *is* the richest woman on earth?"

"No idea," I said. "You could buy a lottery ticket." I pulled bacon out of the fridge and dropped several strips in the frying pan.

"Even Rudy doesn't buy lottery tickets anymore. He says he has just as good a chance of winning if he keeps his money in his pocket. Not that he has money in his pocket."

By the time the bacon was crisp, we had the bread laid out with tomato slices and lettuce. I wrapped the BLTs and put them in a paper sack. "Let's go see if Betina learned anything from cozying up to Woodley."

We walked out to the driveway and I insisted on driving. "You sit in the back seat and pretend you're the richest woman on earth," I suggested. And she did.

"To the salon, Jefferies." She called out from the back seat.

I drove straight up Tennessee Street to town, past the crime scene. The sawhorses had been moved off the road, and traffic was back to its usual trickle. Everybody in town had driven past the scene 20 or 30 times, and that many looks at nothing were sufficient even for people who lived in Knockemstiff.

Pete saw us as I was parking the car and figured immediately why Nellie was in the back seat. He opened the car door for her and stood ramrod straight as she got out. "Good morning, Ms. Phlint," he said.

"Morning, Dawson. Be a dear, won't you, and brew me a cappuccino?"

"Right away, Ms. Phlint. Would you like caviar with that?"

"Fish roe? Don't be disgusting, Dawson."

"No, Ma'am."

"Perhaps a Ding Dong or a Moon Pie would suffice."

"Yes, Ma'am."

"Good morning, Pete," I said.

"Howdy, Savannah," he said.

Betina came in at the same time as our first couple of clients, so we didn't get to hear privately what she had learned from Woodley. I wasn't sure what was safe to ask in front of other people, so I went with a social line of questioning.

"Did you and Investigator Woodley enjoy open mic?"

"We did as a matter of fact."

Betina was coloring Margie's hair — Margie, the waitress at the Bacon Up, who had seen how happy I'd been to get Woodley away from me. Margie's head jerked slightly in surprise at the news that Betina had ended up with Woodley for the evening. Betina barely noticed.

"Easy there, Margie," she said. "You know, he's a much more sophisticated man than he seems at first. I learned so much."

Did she mean she found out something about August?

"He listens to jazz, mostly, but he has a deep appreciation for the delta blues, the tradition and everything. Anyway, he thought Leander was extraordinary. That's the word he used, 'extraordinary.' We all knew that Leander was good, but who knew that he was extraordinary?"

Betina continued rattling on about the blues, and Leander's vocal technique, his guitar playing, his grunting and foot stomping. It was highly authentic, according to Woodley. We were all impressed with how much Betina had learned about the blues — way more than any of the rest of us wanted to know.

When she wound down after a while, Margie asked if she had taken a liking to Woodley.

"Well," she said, as though this was the first time she had considered whether she liked Woodley, "he's got to get rid of that sport coat. But I guess he has a lean kind of look that works with a rumpled jacket, even though that's not really my thing."

She went on talking about Woodley's looks, his hair, and his intense way of looking at you. Pete was looking baffled by this charmed appraisal of the murder investigator who was twice her age. I think we were all looking like that.

Then Betina said, "He can be a little rough."

Pete's eyebrows rocketed up.

"I guess you could say at the end of the night I played good cop, and he played bad cop," she concluded.

"Oooo," Margie said in a pained way.

"Am I getting chemicals in your eyes, Margie?" Betina asked, looking around at Margie's face.

"I'm fine, hon," Margie said. "Just got a little cramp in my groin."

A couple of people cleared their throats. Did Betina have any idea what good cop/bad cop could be about? When she said that Woodley could be rough, did she mean rough around the edges? Or something else?

After a moment, Nellie asked if Betina had learned anything about the investigation.

"Oh, yes," she said. "We talked about that. He told me they're discovering a lot about the case, mainly about the people involved."

"Which people?" Nellie asked.

"He said the obvious ones. I asked, 'like August?' And he said, yes, she was obviously involved, and they are following up several leads. And he was very interested in everything I had to say about August. He really pays attention when you say something."

"He was interested in what *you* had to say about August?" Nellie asked, slightly confused.

"Yes, Nellie," Betina said. "I know you don't think I know a lot, but I might know more than you think. I remember a lot about people that's useful to an investigator."

Did she remember that she was talking to Woodley so she could find out what *he* knew about August?

"I told Investigator Woodley about how August and I double dated, and how August just wasn't interested in boys, so far as I could see. He said that some women were impatient with boys. I agreed with that, for sure. He asked about what August had done in high school, what her activities were, her interests, movies she liked, specific actors even, all kinds of things."

Betina angled her gaze toward Nellie and said, "He was very interested in everything I had to say."

"Sounds that way," said Nellie.

Margie said that it was nice the weather had cooled off a bit. Somebody said the spring has been wet but also hot, so it was nice to get a break. We talked about fascinating items like that until the middle of the afternoon, when Nadine Hines, Chief Tanner's part-time secretary — administrative assistant, Nadine called it — came in for a haircut.

"I've never seen the like of it," she said. That was the most common observation about the goings-on in Knockemstiff this week. She went on to confirm the new view of Annie: she had been a devil.

"Investigator Woodley and the sheriff's deputies have found a number of people who Annie tormented in various ways over the years," Nadine said. "She damaged their property, like with the broken windows. She was handing out false information to patients at the doctor's office."

We knew about that one.

"You know old Mrs. Toler?" Nadine asked. Only a couple of us knew her. She lived alone just outside town and had always been a recluse. "Annie told her that her diabetes was much better and that she could cut back on her insulin to save money."

"She could have died!" said Betina.

"She almost did," Nadine said. "The 'mistake' was discovered by someone. I don't know who."

"She's always been so crotchety, I don't think she gets many visitors," Nellie said.

"Mrs. Toler was lucky. Old Man Feazel wasn't so lucky."

"She killed him?" several people asked at once.

"No, no, his dog," Nadine clarified. "She threatened repeatedly to kill Feazel's dog, according to what he told a deputy, and then he found the dog poisoned. He knew the dog had been poisoned because he found a can of rat poison and some half-eaten hamburger meat next to the body."

Everybody in the salon thought that killing the dog was about as bad as killing a person.

"Why didn't we know these things about Annie until now?" asked Dolores Pettigrew, who was sitting in the café area. Dolores had a hard time adjusting to the fact that she had not known everything about everyone in Knockemstiff.

"Annie knew people well enough to know who she could torment without everyone else finding out," said Nadine. "Apparently, she picked on people who were a little isolated socially for any number of reasons."

"And Woodley thinks that one of these people killed Annie?" Nellie asked.

"That seems to be the general theory," Nadine said. "The problem is, she hurt so many people, the list of suspects is long. And it keeps getting longer. And because these people hardly ever told anyone what Annie was doing, lots more of them could be out there, and how would anyone know? Chief Tanner says that the murderer could be some person we don't see much of in town, somebody who lives way out the Saukum Road or down on the bayou."

Perfect, I thought. That somebody down on the bayou would be Rudy's granddaddy. Was that little encounter he'd had with Annie on Tuesday the first time they'd met? What if Annie had already been tormenting him, and that was just the latest incident – the last straw that caused him to kill Annie?

If he wasn't Nellie's relation, we could report the incident to Woodley and let him follow up. As it was, we'd have to do a little checking ourselves. As I drove us home that evening, with Nellie in the front seat this time ("I sat in the back seat as long as I wanted," she said), we agreed that we needed to find out what was going on with the people down at the swampy end of the bayou.

Chapter 10

We got up Saturday before dawn. The weather looked like it would continue clear, which was good because the roads at the swampy end of the bayou were even more swampy in the rain. They could be treacherous, even with Nellie's 4-wheel drive. We packed a lunch and brought her suitcase-sized first aid kit.

We headed west out of town and turned south on the Old Paudy Highway, which ran roughly parallel to the bayou. The south end of the Knockemstiff Bayou was more than 50 miles from town. It was hard to tell exactly how far it was to the south end because the bayou gradually turned into a swamp that went on for miles. Where did the bayou end and the swamp begin?

As the sun was just peeking up in the east, we talked about what we knew.

"Not much," Nellie summarized before we started.

"There's your optimistic outlook again," I said. I thought about how little we knew. "I share your optimism."

"With the possible exception of Rudy's granddaddy," Nellie said, "none of the suspects we've heard about seems capable of killing anybody."

"We don't really know some of these people very well," I said. "I mean, we've known Mr. Keshian for ages, but we don't really know him. I don't even know his first name."

"We don't know other first names," Nellie pointed out logically. "That doesn't keep us from trusting Mr. Coffee and Mr. Goodbar."

"What about Old Man Feazel?" I countered. "Do we trust him? A man who's been taunted and had his dog murdered could do anything. Also I'm guessing that 'Old Man' is not his real first name."

"An obvious pseudonym," Nellie said.

I turned in my seat to look at her. "I would not have guessed that you knew that word."

"Many people have jumped to the conclusion that I'm not very bright just because I've done so many stupid things," she said.

I put my hand on her arm. "Seriously, Nellie, I think you're smarter than you look."

"While we're talking seriously," she said, "let's seriously consider that we can't imagine Old Man Feazel killing anyone. And we can't imagine anyone else we know killing anyone."

"OK, so we have lousy imaginations," I admitted, "which is why we're talking about what we know, like they do on TV, so we can figure out the known knowns and the unknown unknowns and like that."

"OK," Nellie said, "what about the Paramabets? We've only known them approximately forever, and we don't know their first names. That little one who takes care of the cash drawer could be killer material."

"There you go. Now we're getting somewhere. When I pay for a taco, the gleam in his 9-year-old eyes is sharp as tacks. Count your change."

"So we're back to having no one to suspect."

"With the possible exception of Rudy's granddaddy," I said. Then I named the person we'd been trying to avoid naming. "And August?"

"August as a murderer?" Nellie said.

"Isn't it suspicious that she's disappeared?"

"*Seems* to have disappeared. And having SLUT painted on your windshield doesn't seem like the sort of thing you'd kill a person for. I mean, if you're the kind of person who would feel that wounded by being called a slut, are you the kind of person who would go shoot somebody?"

"So you figure that you have to be an outgoing personality type to shoot somebody?" I wondered.

"Let's try to imagine a shy, retiring slip of a girl using a thirty-ought-six at close range."

We drove in silence for a couple of minutes. The sun was well up, and we were driving past a field planted with some kind of low-growing crop. Soybeans? When I used to ride in the car with my parents, they would comment on all the crops. "The corn isn't very high for this time of year," they'd say. Or "nice-looking alfalfa." I assumed that when I got to be an adult, I'd know everything about crops, too. That's the kind of thing that adults knew. I didn't.

On the other side of the road was a line of scraggly trees and bushes, then a tiny cemetery with no fence around it. We crossed a creek that was full from the rain earlier in the week. A white cattle egret flew up from the creek bank as we drove past.

"Maybe we just have lousy imaginations," I said. Again. "Or maybe we don't know everything that Annie did to August. From what we've heard, Annie tormented some people for years. What if the SLUT thing was only the latest insult? What if it drove August bonkers?"

"What if it drives us bonkers?" Nellie said.

We went over another creek that broadened into a swampy area on the right side of the road. We were passing fewer fields and more stretches of road that were lined with trees on both sides. We went by a dirt road marked with a homemade sign that said "Moody."

Another mile or so on, we passed a cinder block building that had once been painted white. The windows had disappeared long ago, and vines were growing up the sides of the building and across the gravel parking area. Hanging from the front was a rusted sign that said "Henry's."

"Did you know that place?" I asked.

"It was open when I married Rudy, when he brought me down here for the first time. I don't remember when it closed."

"Well, that liquor store was the only business around here for a long, long time." I said. "When I was very young, there was a wooden building there. At some point it burned, and only a brick chimney was left standing. Then they built this cinder block thing."

"How do you come to know so much about this part of the country?" Nellie asked with some surprise.

"My parents loved to drive all over the place," I said. "On any given Sunday, we'd drive out to a far corner of the parish or over to the Atchafalaya. I thought it was so much fun just to go for a drive."

"The fun part of our little drive is about to start," Nellie said. "Here's our turn."

She slowed to a crawl to make the drop off the pavement onto a dirt track and stopped the SUV.

"How do you know this is the turn?" I asked. "It looks like every other dirt road along here."

"See that live oak along there a little ways? That's our street sign." She got out of the SUV and locked the front wheel hubs.

"Looks like all the other live oaks along here," I said.

"It does, actually, but it happens to be almost exactly a mile and a half from Henry's," Nellie said as she climbed back into the SUV. She engaged the 4WD lever, and we started down the muddy track that ran in the general direction of the bayou. We lurched and splashed through mud puddles and broad washes.

"This is muddier than I expected," I said.

"And this is after it hasn't rained for a couple of days," Nellie said.

The road skirted open boggy areas and hugged the edges of slightly higher ground that was wooded or dense with saw palmetto. Every now and then the twisting track branched, and Nellie took the left or right fork, pointing out some little road mark that reminded her which way to go.

I was getting nervous about getting lost. "How far is it?" I asked.

"We'll be there when we get there," Nellie shouted.

"Seriously, how far is it?" I asked again.

"Seriously, I don't know," she said. "Maybe 10 miles? I don't generally pay much attention to the odometer when —."

Her answer was cut short by a boom near the left side of the SUV, followed by the sound of a pump-action shotgun being pumped and another boom, followed by another pump. Nellie took these shots as a hint that she should stop the SUV. We looked into the dense bushes to the left but couldn't see anyone.

"Run for it?" I asked.

"No way in this place," she said. "Maybe I made a wrong turn."

She rolled her window down. As soon as the window was all the way down, a woman called out with one of those voices that a dog would not dream of disobeying, "Let's see your hands."

We raised our hands as Nellie called back, "Sorry if we're trespassing. We're trying to find Horace Conway Phlint. Could you tell us which way we should be going?"

At that, a huge old woman in a blue dress with little pink flowers on it stepped from behind a scrub oak pointing the shotgun directly at us.

"Who are you?" she asked, squinting in the bright sunlight. Before Nellie could answer, the woman said, "Nellie? Is that you?"

"Nellie, yes, Aunt Hattie. It's me."

"Nellie, it's so nice to see you."

"Nice to see you too, Aunt Hattie."

"Who you got with you there, Nellie?" she asked, gesturing in my direction with the shotgun.

"This is my friend, Savannah Jefferies. I work in her hair salon. The Teasen and

Pleasen?"

"Jefferies? You Ellis Jefferies girl?"

"Yes, Ma'am," I answered.

"Well do tell," Hattie said. "How is your daddy?"

"He passed away four years ago this fall," I said. "His heart."

"Sorry to hear that," Hattie said. "My, my, what a character he was." She lowered the shotgun as she looked down and shook her head. "What a character."

Nellie and I tentatively lowered our hands.

"Well, it's a pleasure to meet you, Savannah Jefferies," Hattie said.

"Pleasure to meet you, Aunt Hattie," I lied.

She came out of the bushes and put her hand on the window frame of the SUV, peering in at me. "You do favor Ellis, child. I can see his eyes right there on your pretty face." She patted the window frame and repeated, "Right there."

Hattie looked at Nellie. "What brings your girls way out here to see Conway?"

Of all the things Nellie and I had talked about on the way, we had not taken a moment to come up with a rationale for this visit. *We've come to see if you murdered a woman?*

"Aunt Hattie," Nellie said, "Savannah and I were talking about her family, and about how her mama and daddy have passed, and her grandparents gone years ago, and how she misses having family around her, and I told her that's a shame. Family's one of the most important things we have. And since Rudy's gone with the boys out on the Tickfaw, I thought why not Savannah and I visit some family? Sit and talk, maybe shell some beans?"

Hattie looked at Nellie with amusement in her eyes. "The Tickfaw, you say."

"He went out there earlier in the week," Nellie said.

"I see," Hattie said. "Well, I don't know what you girls are up to, but I don't reckon there's any harm in you passing the time of day with Conway." She took her hand off the window frame and straightened up. "Bear in mind he's got no beans to shell."

She turned and said over her shoulder, "Hold on a second." She walked back into the bushes.

I whispered to Nellie, "She doesn't reckon there's any harm? That's an odd way to put it." I looked out at Hattie in the bushes. "Is she talking into a walkie-talkie?"

"Kinda looks that way," Nellie whispered back.

"Nice line of fluff, by the way."

"She didn't buy it," Nellie whispered.

"I think she was tickled with your efforts," I whispered. "Where did you get the beans?"

Nellie pointed to her head.

Hattie came back toward us with the shotgun on her shoulder. "Sorry about the 12-gauge," she said. "We get too many varmints in here joyriding." She opened the rear door and got in. "Ease on down to your left there and then around to the right. I'll show you a shortcut."

Nellie guided the SUV off the track we'd been following, through an axle-deep wallow, and around the little stand of scrub oaks that Hattie had been hiding in. Soon we found ourselves on a hard-pack surface that was more or less even and free from major potholes.

We rolled along in silence for a couple of minutes until Hattie said, "Stop here, Nellie."

Hattie got out and walked about 10 yards along the road to where some rusty barbed wire was tangled around a fallen tree. With one hand she lifted the end of the tree trunk and walked it out into the road in front of us. We could see now that the trunk was balanced on a pivot that made it easy to move. Hattie motioned us through the opening where the tree trunk had been.

When Nellie had driven through, Hattie pulled the tree bunk back into place and got back in. "All right, Savannah, welcome to Phlint Swamp."

We rolled along the road for another 50 yards or so, and then the solid ground fell away on either side. We were surrounded by cypress swamp. The road wound among the huge trunks and knees of the bald cypress trees, with cascades of Spanish moss hanging from the branches overhead in gray-green curtains. The sun glinted here and there off the water. It was absolutely beautiful.

We wound in and out of the cypresses for a while and then pulled into a small clearing, where the weedy hulks of two pickup trucks and a tractor sat rusting in front of a grey-shingled shack built on stilts at the edge of a patch of open water. Several sets of deer antlers were mounted on the side of the shack, along with some large fish heads, bleached white by the sun.

As we got out of the SUV, an old man came out onto the front porch and let the screen door slam shut behind him. "Nellie," he said. "Come on in the house."

Now that we were out of the SUV's air conditioning, an odor of dank, fungousy decay hung over everything, making the air seem thick, almost liquid. I could hear bugs humming and buzzing all around and swatted at a horsefly that landed on my arm. I walked up the wooden steps behind Nellie.

"You must be Savannah," the old man said to me.

"You must be Rudy's granddaddy," I said. How did he know who I was? "Have we met?"

"Yeah, yeah," he said. "You've done some growing since then." He opened the screen door and motioned us inside. He was wearing Dickies bib overalls over a T-shirt that he had on inside-out.

"Will you come in, Hattie?" he asked. "Join us for something cold."

"Believe I will have a sip," Hattie said.

"Ya'll go on around to the shady porch," Conway said.

Hattie led Nellie and I past the kitchen and through a shabby living room to a screened porch that faced onto the bayou and the cypress swamp. A hound dog lifted his head and looked at us with mild interest.

"Ya'll make yourselves at home," Hattie said. She shuffled back to the kitchen.

Nellie and I looked at each other, and I could see that she was as confused as I was. Something wasn't right. This situation was too well put together.

"He doesn't seem dangerous," I whispered. "And he has teeth."

"I don't know where he got them," Nellie whispered.

We both shrugged and sat down in wicker rocking chairs. The dog put his head back down on his paws and continued to watch us. We looked out at the bayou. We could see a stretch of open water and a small dock with a row boat tied up.

In a few minutes Hattie returned with a pitcher of sweet tea and a couple of glasses filled with ice cubes. "You take lemon in your tea?" she asked.

"Please Ma'am," Nellie said. I nodded.

She disappeared again. She returned with lemon wedges in an ancient crockery bowl and two more glasses. Conway came in with a plastic container of Girl Scout cookies.

Nellie laughed. "Daddy Phlint, the Girl Scouts find you way out here?"

"If you ever get lost," he said. "Just wait and them scouts will find you. But somebody brung us these from Paudy." He sat down in a rocker. "Sorry they're cold. If we don't keep 'em in the refrigerator, they grow stiff pretty quick."

Hattie poured the tea in our glasses. We sat and rocked and sipped our tea for a minute.

"It's good of you girls to come see us," Conway said.

Nellie cleared her throat. "I reckon you're wondering why we came out here."

Conway took a cookie out of the container and looked at her. The dog lifted his head and looked at the cookie. Conway bit the cookie in half and chewed, and then put the rest of the cookie in his mouth. The dog put his head back down on his paws.

"It's just that we're trying to find out about somebody in Knockemstiff," Nellie said, "somebody who *was* in Knockemstiff, who you might know." She took a sip of her tea.

Conway took a sip of his tea.

"I saw you in town last week," she said, "so I thought you might know something." She sipped more tea. "About Annie Simmerson."

Conway stopped chewing. "What about her?" he asked.

"You probably haven't heard out here," Nellie said, "but she was shot last week."

Conway started chewing again. "That's good," he said.

"She was murdered," I said.

"Glad to hear it," he said evenly.

"So you know her? Knew her?" Nellie asked.

"Why are you asking me this, Nellie?"

"We're worried about a murderer on the loose," I answered. "And we're also finding out that Annie was a bad person. So we're trying to understand what's going on."

"She was a witch," he said. "I knew her. Way out here, I knew what she was. I know people she was torturing." He stood up and glared at us. I wondered if the knife was about to come out.

"Now you tell me something," he said to us. "How is it that you people in town didn't know what she was? You people who were around her every day? How is it you let her go on hurting people for so long?"

"We didn't know, Daddy Phlint," Nellie said. "She was nice to us."

"Blast it!" He shouted, stomping the floor. "Nice?"

"Now mind your blood pressure, Conway," Hattie said.

The dog got up and sidled out into the living room.

"It's past now," Hattie said. "Somebody dealt with the woman."

"Well," Conway said. He sat down in the rocker. Then he turned toward Nellie again. "I still don't understand why you are talking to me. You say you saw me in town?"

"I saw you bump into Annie," Nellie said. "With something long and heavy in your gunny sack."

He continued to look at her quizzically.

"She said something to you, and you said something back. You seemed upset."

"At the hardware store," he said. "Yes. She said she knew about… something I was doing."

He stopped and thought for a moment. "You think I had a rifle in my gunny sack. You think I shot her, don't you?"

"We're just trying to find out who knows what, Mr. Phlint," I said. "We're just trying to understand."

"Well, understand that I had a length of steel pipe in my gunny sack. I was hoping Botowski Hardware could get me more pipe just like it." He stood up again. "And understand that I never shot nobody who wasn't cheating at cards."

That's when we heard a noise that sounded like an airplane landing out on the bayou and Rudy cruised up to the dock on an air boat.

Chapter 11

Rudy shut down the engine on the air boat, and the big propeller at the back slowed to a stop. He took off his ear muffs and goggles and looked up at the house. Nellie stood up and stared down at Rudy in disbelief. He began tying off the boat. Clearly he hadn't seen Nellie or he would have restarted the air boat in reverse immediately.

"I thought you said he'd be staying at the shed overnight," Conway said to Hattie.

"Reckon not," she said.

Rudy picked up a knapsack and a rifle from the boat and stepped onto the dock. He walked to the side of the house and came up the back steps. Nellie met him at the top.

"Tickfaw, Rudy. You are on the Tickfaw River," she said.

He looked up at her with his mouth open.

"Is this the Tickfaw River? *This* is not the Tickfaw River, Rudy. This is the Knockemstiff bayou. This is one hundred *bless*ed miles from the Tickfaw."

"Ah," he said.

"Where are the boys, Rudy?"

"Ah, the boys are on the Tickfaw, Sugar."

"The boys are a hundred miles away on the Tickfaw. In the swamp. By. Them. Selves. Is that right?"

"Well, they're in a state park campground. They're all right. They have free Wi-Fi."

Nellie stood there for a moment. I knew she was picturing Dale, her youngest, wandering around the swamp with both alligators and crocodiles close behind him.

"Is someone looking after them, Rudy?"

"They're fine, Sugar. They can look after themselves. I left them the four-ten."

"Good, Rudy. The four-ten. They can defend themselves if they get attacked by a bunny rabbit." She turned and slammed the heel of her hand against the side of the house.

"Come on inside," Rudy said. He took her hand to see how much damage she'd done to it. She snatched it away from him.

"Let me explain," he said. "I was saving it for a surprise."

I thought he had managed to surprise her pretty well.

Rudy saw me as they came up onto the screened porch. His mouth dropped open slightly again, but he was just about surprised-out from seeing Nellie.

"Hey Savannah," he said.

"Hey Rudy."

"What're you all doing out here?" he asked.

"Road trip," I said.

"I see," he said. He exchanged heys with Hattie and Conway.

Hattie said, "I would of called you, but I thought you were staying there."

"Forgot my phone," he said.

"You have a connection way out here?" I asked.

"No, no," Rudy said. "It's useless as a phone. I play games on it."

Then how could Hattie call him, I wondered. Walkie-talkie? But Nellie was fuming and impatient to hear what Rudy thought he was doing. Rudy told his grandfather and Aunt Hattie that it was time to show us *Barn 2*.

The way he said *Barn 2* made me think it was one of those places that once they show you, they have to shoot you. Something about staring down the barrel of Hattie's 12-gauge had made me even less curious than I might normally have been. I've seen lots of barns. None of them was worth getting shot for.

Still, I didn't feel like I was in a position to say "No, thank you." Nellie was on Rudy's heels as he went out the back door, demanding to know if this *barn* somehow justified abandoning their children by the Tickfaw River. Rudy would only say, "You'll see, you'll see." He was leading us down to the dock.

"You know," Hattie called out from the top of the steps. "Barn 2 will only make sense if you show them the original."

"Yeah," Rudy said after a pause. "Ask Granddaddy is it OK, and I'll take them over there."

"It's his idea," she said. "I'll bring the keys. Meet you at the front door."

We walked around to the front of the house, where Hattie was coming down the front steps. We walked past the rusted tractor, around a stand of pines, past several submarine-shaped propane tanks, and found ourselves at a corrugated tin barn that looked about as old and operational as the tractor hulk next to the house.

Hattie unlocked three locks on a small side door, and we went into an open barn containing a number of 55-gallon drums, two larger drum-shaped tanks and lots of metal tubing. But the most noticeable thing in the barn was the overwhelming odor of smelly feet.

"Do you have secret gym classes in here?" I asked.

Hattie didn't even laugh. "That's what it smells like, all right. You should smell it when it's cooking."

"Moonshine," said Nellie, glaring at Rudy.

"I knew you'd get it," Rudy said a little more brightly than seemed warranted.

He explained to me that one of Nellie's uncles had been a moonshiner. Nellie had visited the still when she was a girl and grown up seeing the effects of "white liquor" on family members. When Rudy had found out after they were married, he knew it would be a good idea to keep Nellie away from his granddaddy's place, so his granddaddy had gone back to behaving like his river-barge deckhand self to discourage family visits.

"Wait a minute," Nellie said. "That scary-granddaddy thing was an act?"

At this Hattie did laugh. "I wish. Conway was always scary. He *had* wore out on it over the years. When you were around, he just let himself go more."

"I had to come visit in secret," Rudy said.

"So this is where you were always running off to," Nellie said.

"Right," Rudy said, as if it had just occurred to him that this could account for all his gallivanting.

He explained that he had helped his granddaddy work the still over the years. "All that time you thought I wasn't working, I was applying myself to upgrade the product."

"So I should be proud of you," Nellie said. "For moonshining."

Rudy let that comment bounce off and went on with his story. Before Prohibition, this still had been in town. In fact, the original name of the Knockemback Tavern had been the Knockemback Bar and Still. The Phlints had been known as local corn-whisky makers who were making a product a cut above the people like Nellie's uncle who used old car radiators and whatnot in their stills.

"So I should be proud of you," Nellie said, "for not giving people lead poisoning."

Rudy let that comment bounce off as well. He was maintaining a remarkably cheerful attitude in the face of a bad situation. He went on with his story.

"Lately we've come up with some pretty good ideas. Granddaddy always thought that white liquor could be as good as any other whiskey if he could push it a little. He could never make his mind up whether he wanted to push it toward bourbon or gin, so he experimented with both ways. We couldn't afford oak barrels, so bourbon seemed out of reach until I realized we could get the oak in another way."

He was clearly dazzled by his own creativity here. Even Nellie was becoming interested in the story.

"We cut up live oak branches and let them dry next to the propane flame that heats the still. Then we put the dried pieces of oak in 55-gallon drums with the white liquor and let it age. It wasn't bourbon, but it wasn't half bad. We called it Oak Kool-Aid."

At the same time, Rudy's granddaddy had been trying out local plants to see if any of them gave the liquor an interesting taste. He would toss in handfuls of whatever bushes he found growing around the bayou. Gradually he decided that a half dozen of them made him happy. He and Rudy combined the bush-flavored liquor with Oak Kool-Aid, and a star was born: Bayou Shine.

"At last year's American Alcohol Association conference, Bayou Shine won an Artisanal Spirits Star award."

"Rudy, that spells ASS," Nellie said.

Rudy grinned. "Yes, that's an inside joke."

"It's not inside anything, Rudy. It's hanging out there mooning anybody who cares to look. If it's real."

Hattie said, "It's real, all right. We're not just 'shiners. We're distillers of artisanal spirits. And you haven't heard the best part."

Rudy said he ought to *show* us the best part. He led us back toward the house, explaining that we needed to go for a little boat ride.

As we approached the front steps, Conway was coming down holding a mason jar half full of greenish-brown liquid. It looked like bayou water. "It's bad luck to look at a still without trying the liquor," he said.

"He made up that line a while back," Hattie said, "so we'd have a good reason to take a sip every time we tended the still. Not that we were needing a good reason."

She unscrewed the lid of the jar and handed it to Nellie, who sipped cautiously. Her eyebrows went up and she worked her mouth a little. She handed the jar to me. Was this really safe? I sipped anyway. My eyebrows went up. I worked my mouth a little. I'd never tasted anything like it, and it wasn't half bad. We passed the jar around a couple of times. I was starting to think this might be the first hard liquor I'd tasted that I might like.

"Impressed?" Conway asked. "See, we folks out here on the bayou might be poor, but we rich in spirits." He cackled at his well-practiced joke.

As we walked around to the dock, Rudy told us that they had been selling lots of Bayou Shine on the Internet. "Norris came up with a great description for our web site: Artisanal spirits aged in oak with 16 botanicals unique to the Louisiana bayou." Norris was their middle boy.

"You have a web site?" Nellie asked.

"Norris and Aubrey manage that," Rudy said, "and they're running a great social media campaign. They must have a thousand different identities that drive traffic to our site."

"I don't have a clue what you just said except that you seem to be saying that our sons are participating in the commission of a felony. Selling moonshine is a felony, I think?"

"Felony, yes," Rudy confirmed breezily, "but only temporarily. Here." He handed Nellie and I ear muffs and goggles and started the air boat's engine.

The boat had only one proper seat, so Nellie and I sat on flotation cushions and held on to cleats in the bottom of the boat. In a minute we were waving goodbye to Hattie and blasting across the surface of the bayou, the propeller making a tremendous noise even through the ear muffs.

We went around a stand of bald cypress and through a grassy area, where it was hard to see that there was enough water even for the flat-bottomed air boat. 15 minutes later we skirted another stand of cypress and arrived at a floating dock.

After walking through a grove of live oak, we came to a clearing and saw maybe 20 enormous mirrors surrounding a corrugated-tin building and a very, very bright light.

"Best to not look directly at it," Rudy said. "The mirrors direct sunlight onto a tower on top of the barn. This was Aubrey's idea, by the way."

"This is a solar power generator?" Nellie asked.

"Sort of."

We went around the mirrors and into the building, where we saw lots and lots of steel pipes and tanks, all spotless and new. The only sound was from electric motors, obviously driving pumps. The dirty-feet smell was powerful here. This was a second still.

Rudy looked up toward one end of the space and waved at someone in a glassed-in booth. "Cousin Roebuck," he said. Roebuck waved back. "Granddaddy let him know we were coming. He's putting the new still through its paces."

"This is a solar-powered still." I said. It was amazing.

"Aubrey calls it the most technologically advanced moonshine still in America," Rudy said. "Technically, that's only true for another week. In about seven days, we should get our license. We'll no longer be 'shiners. We'll be artisanal distillers."

***

As we were driving home, Nellie said that this had been the weirdest day of her life. Possibly because it was so weird, she allowed Rudy to talk her into letting the boys stay on the Tickfaw for another few days, even though she really thought she should drive straight over there and fetch them home.

I agreed that the day had been exceedingly weird. And it all came about because we were looking for information about a murder. We were no closer to figuring that out, were we?

We were pretty sure that Rudy's granddaddy hadn't shot Annie, but Rudy had said something disturbing when Nellie had told him in a private moment why we came. Rudy had gotten agitated and pooh-poohed the idea that Conway could have murdered Annie.

"He's just not that out of control these days," Rudy had said. "I mean, she somehow knew what we were doing out here — that woman was a fiend, and she knew all kinds of things she used to torment people — but we didn't have anything to do with getting rid of her."

"It wasn't entirely convincing," Nellie said.

Chapter 12

After our weird day in the swamp, Nellie was delighted to help me weed the garden. It's amazing how "down to earth" you can get when you weed a garden. It made the episode in the swamp seem more unreal than it had at the time. It also made Nellie feel that it was crazy to allow her boys to stay at the Tickfaw River by themselves.

I offered to drive with her to get them, but she said she could use the time to think. "Besides, you need to invite Connor for dinner," she said. While we were weeding, I'd told her about my thought earlier in the week to invite him. That thought occurred to me a few minutes before I found Annie dead. That seemed like a long time ago.

After Nellie left, I phoned Connor, who sounded pretty down — as blue as he'd been when he read his homesick poem at open mic. He thanked me for the dinner invitation but declined, saying that his hound Finnegan was doing poorly so he didn't want to leave him alone.

I suppose I should have taken his excuse as a way of saying "I don't want to have dinner with you." And I suppose I'm a *little* pushy because I more or less insisted that I bring veggies from my garden and cook dinner for him at his place. I felt like he needed better company than Finnegan. While I'm supposing, I guess I have to suppose that I see myself as better company than a dog. That may be the human conceit that often makes dogs better company than people.

In any case, I told him that I had a couple of garden tools that needed sharpening, and he said he'd be glad to do that. He sounded more enthusiastic about dealing with the tools than with me. I consoled myself with the thought that a dog wouldn't bring him tools to sharpen. Dinner and tools — what could make for better company than that?

These things didn't put Connor in his happy place, however and I underestimated how down he was. He was in what my ex called bottomless funk or funk all the way down.

I promised myself I wouldn't try to make him talk. While I fixed dinner, he sharpened my pruning sheers and edging tool.

Over dinner he suggested that I get one of those electric edgers. "It would save a lot of work," he said.

"And make a lot of noise," I said. "When I'm doing yard work, I'm happy doing the work. I wouldn't give up my mower, but everything else needs to be quiet. And I got that edger from my daddy. Can't give that up."

"I wondered how old it was. It'll need a new handle in a few years, but if it's sharpened without taking too much edge off, it should last another 50, maybe 70 years."

I told him that he was my man to sharpen it. Then I thought he said, "Or you could find someone good." But he had mumbled in his heavy Irish accent with his head down as he got up and left the room.

I kicked myself under the table. The "sharpen my tool" thing must have been over the top. After he came back he apologized.

"Sorry," he said. "Thought I heard Finnegan." He sat down and went back to picking at his chicken creole.

"What's wrong with Finnegan? Did you take him to the vet?"

"I know what's wrong. Didn't need the vet. Finnegan was poisoned."

"No! Old Man Feazel's dog was poisoned by Annie Simmerson," I said.

"Who also poisoned Finnegan," he said.

"Connor, that's terrible. It's unbelievable. How could a person do these things?"

He kept chewing a bite of chicken with his head down. I studied his wild mop of red hair. His might have been the only tousled head of hair I've never wanted to tame.

After a moment I realized he was struggling not to cry.

"Oh, Connor," I said and went over to put my arms around him.

After a moment he echoed my words: "How could a person do these things?" He stopped chewing and took a gulp of water. "How could she do these things after she was so sweet to me? After we were so close?"

Huh? How close was that? I wanted to ask. Had Connor had a thing for sweet little Annie? Had she had a thing for big rough Connor? Had they had a thing together? I couldn't help wondering what I might expect from a relationship with Connor if he was into *things* with women half my age.

I felt like hitting him. My daddy taught me that violence never solves anything, so I kissed the little balding spot on the top of Connor's head instead. That made me feel stupid. I tried to think of something smart to do. Leave? Good grief! I'm like a walking doofus around this guy.

"We all thought Annie was sweet," I said automatically. I straightened up and walked to the sink and started rattling dishes.

"August was never fooled," he said. "She warned me that Annie was trouble."

"So August knew?" Great, I thought, another girl half my age. Did Connor collect them?

"A long time ago," Connor said. "And she told me over and over. So many times. If I'd listened to her back then, many bad things would not have happened."

How could this man have been around August "so many times"? And what did "a long time ago" mean? Just a couple of years before, August had been in high school.

"Connor, do you know where August is? Betina doesn't know where she is, and she's worried about her."

"Fehh," Connor said. "Betina doesn't know anything."

"Connor! I work with Betina every day. What are you saying?"

"Sorry, sorry," he said, holding up his hands. "I just mean that things have been going on in this town for so long, and nobody has been willing to see."

"The things that Annie did?"

"Yes!"

"And Betina could have known?"

"Look," Connor said, "I'm just saying that Betina doesn't know everything she thinks she knows. And I'm saying that *everyone* should have seen what Annie was about."

"Including you."

"Yes."

"And all the time August knew. And she was telling you and no one else. For some reason?"

He let out a breath. He looked stunned, like he'd finally realized what he'd been talking about. But what had he been talking about?

"Connor, I'd better get going. I'll just say bye to Finnegan."

I went around to the utility room where Finnegan was lying in his doggie bed. I'd wanted to walk straight out the door. I don't know why I didn't. I felt like I didn't want to see Connor again. I was so confused.

I sat on the floor and petted Finnegan for a couple of minutes while I collected my thoughts. Connor banged plates and pots in the kitchen. Finnegan wagged his tail in a feeble way. Poor baby.

As I stroked the dog's head and tried to think straight, I noticed a flowery piece of clothing hanging behind the door. This was Connor's laundry room, but this didn't look like something Connor would wear.

I stood up and swung the door aside so I could see that it was exactly what it looked like: a little sun dress. And when I say little, I mean much shorter than anything Betina would wear, much shorter than any woman could conceivably wear in this town.

For a moment I thought it might be a child's dress, but the neckline plunging nearly to the waist made it unmistakable. This was a slut dress.

Chapter 13

Monday morning was overcast, threatening rain. My thoughts were still in a whirl as I drove to the salon, but I'd calmed down about whatever was going on with Connor. He could mix it up with any young women who wanted to mix it up with him. It hurt my feelings and disappointed me, but it was none of my business.

Nellie helped calm me down when we talked on the phone Sunday night. She disagreed that what I'd found was a slut dress. She said, "If a woman wears it around the house, it's not a slut dress, it's lingerie."

She had found the boys in the Tickfaw campground having a great time. They made friends with a family from Shreveport who were camping and nobody had any permanent injuries.

Her two older boys raised a ruckus over her assumption that they were all going back home. They told her their Internet connection at home sucked. "That's the technical term for it, Ma: sucks."

They were beside themselves trying to explain why the Tickfaw campground's excellent Wi-Fi was so important until she told them that she knew about the moonshining. Then they exclaimed about how "vital" it was to "relaunch the product" and other activities that she didn't understand. They said that their mother should not "squash their entrepreneurial spirit."

At the end of the day, literally, she brought the youngest boy home and left the other two. That plan had not been popular either, but she avoided mutiny by promising to bring little Dale back to the campground the next weekend. It turned out he thought the weekend was coming up in a couple of days, and Nellie didn't correct the mistake. "It's about time he learned what day of the week it is," she said.

Now we were ready to cut hair on a Monday morning. We didn't feel like we knew any more about Annie's murderer, but we knew a lot more about everybody else. More than I wanted to know about some people.

First up for Betina was the Bald Eagle, who came in every Monday morning mainly to hear about whatever Betina had been up to over the weekend. While he enjoyed the gab fest, he would get a wash and trim, even though he didn't have much left to trim.

The Eagle was up front about his missing hair. Each week Betina began by asking him if he wanted a Brazilian blow-out, to which the Eagle replied that he didn't have time today, "Just a little off the sides, please."

This week, as Betina shampooed his cranium, the Eagle was disappointed that she failed to begin with either date-night tales or the Brazilian blow-out line. Instead, she asked him, "Sanders, have you seen August lately? I don't know where she is."

Caught off guard, the Eagle answered, "Why would you think I know where August is?"

"Sanders, you live next door to her. You see her come and go, don't you?"

"Right," he confessed.

"Well, have you seen her lately?" Betina was massaging the shampoo around his head, which usually sent the Eagle into a state of suspended animation. She might have gotten better results if she'd waited until she had him under her scissors. As it was, he said he didn't know anything about August or what she was up to, if anything.

It was an unusually slow Monday. Nellie and I were full of moonshining news that would inflate into amazing gossip in two shakes of a lamb's tail if we dared talk about it. The need to maintain secrecy weighed heavily on us, so we hardly said anything all morning.

It didn't help that the fishwife who lived out on the bayou was back in, the one who had theorized that aliens were behind all the window breaking and spray painting. She reported that she and her husband continued to see strange lights out on the southern end of the bayou. They heard strange aircraft noises too.

"Maybe it's just people riding around in air boats," Nellie suggested. I gave her my "Where are you going with that comment?" look, but she wouldn't look at me. She smiled and continued cutting the woman's hair.

The woman said, "As a matter of fact, we have seen people in air boats — if they are people. I don't know what they could be doing. Why would aliens be riding around in air boats?"

A number of people professed complete ignorance of any practical knowledge of air boats and then speculated at length about how they might be used. Ugh! The morning crept by.

Betina, who was largely responsible for providing Monday-morning entertainment at the salon, had stayed home all weekend, "flipping through magazines, washing my hair, doing my nails, flipping out from boredom."

"Anything new in *Seventeen*?" Pete asked, partly as a playful poke at her. At 22, Betina was still "flipping through" *Seventeen* every month.

"Dull, dull, dull," she said. "Peyton Meyer, dull. Liam Hemsworth, dull. Dylan O'Brien, dull. Even Zac Efron, dull."

"Betina, I thought you were nuts about those boys," said Pete, who was a little nuts about those boys himself.

"They're hot," she admitted. "But they didn't do a single interesting thing last month."

Something about this conversation jogged my memory. Hadn't Betina mentioned something about actors last week? Something that Investigator Woodley wanted to know about actors?

"I did see some fascinating facts about Botox in *Nylon*," Betina was saying. "Did you know that Botox injections in your face can help treat depression?"

"My face is the *reason* I'm depressed," said Paulette Strickland, who was at that moment getting a facial from Nellie. Paulette would not be considered beautiful by a casual observer unless she was smiling, which was often the case. She had the most radiant smile for miles around.

"Your face will not be depressing when I get done with it, Paulette," said Nellie. "You'll be smiling all the time."

"Go ahead and shoot in some Botox while you're at it," Paulette said. "Can't hurt."

That led to a discussion of whether it was possible to smile if you had Botox injected in your face. Someone speculated about the frustration of seeing your own beautifully Botoxed face in a mirror and not being able to smile about it.

"I'd be willing to give it a shot," Betina's 11:15 said. "So to speak."

Someone else wondered if anyone in Knockemstiff had ever gotten Botox injections. No one in the salon had. Or at least no one was willing to admit it.

Someone speculated that Dolores Pettigrew was the only person in town likely to have tried it. We agreed that we'd see if we could get her to talk about it. That got a laugh. If there was anything Dolores wasn't willing to talk about, we hadn't found it yet.

Betina also reported from the magazine article that Botox comes from botulism.

"Oh, I've had that," Paulette said. She hadn't been careful about canning some quince jam a couple of years back, and she and her husband had gotten very sick. Dr. Cason had told them they were lucky to pull through. "I guess I should have smeared it on my face than put it in my mouth," Paulette concluded.

Someone wondered if it would be possible to get Dr. Cason to visit the salon once a week for a Botox clinic. Of course that reminded everyone of Dr. Cason's assistant — former assistant — Annie and the fact that she was a devil and had been murdered. After a few minutes of depressed silence in the salon, Paulette observed that we all needed

Botox injections to cheer us up.

Nellie asked if anyone had seen Dr. Cason lately. He didn't seem to be visible around town as much as usual. He was undoubtedly upset by the news about Annie, and without an assistant, he must be overworked. The last time anyone could recall seeing him, he was leaving his office with Connor O'Sullivan. They each had a sheaf of papers, and they drove off in opposite directions. I could only wonder what that was all about.

For the umpteenth time, someone posed the question of whether Annie didn't deserve what she got. By now everyone was convinced that Annie had been a devil, but no one was willing to say out loud that she deserved to be shot.

By the time our late lunch time rolled around, everyone in the café area was happy enough to get out of the salon and move on to anything different. Pete went to the Grosri for something to eat, leaving Betina, Nellie and I huddled in the café area trying to think of something cheerful. Nellie was attacking her sandwich like she was starving.

After a few bites of my salad, I remembered why Betina's comments about actors jogged my memory. She'd said the week before that Woodley asked what movie actors August liked. At the time this struck me as an odd question. I asked Betina if she knew why he wanted to know.

"He is so inquisitive," she said. "He didn't just want to know about August. He asked what I was interested in, too. He wanted to know about everything — movies, actors, magazines." She nibbled on a carrot. "Sports, hobbies." She nibbled the carrot some more. "Preferences in bed." She laughed. "I told him I couldn't tell him *every*thing."

Betina looked at me as she nibbled another carrot. "He also asked about you, by the way."

"About my preferences in bed?" I asked warily.

"Not specifically," she said. "Just general interests, like movies."

"And you told him what?"

"Um, I think I said that you like regular chick flicks, rom coms, movies with strong mature men. Did I get that right?"

"Sure," I said.

"He wanted to know what actors you like. I told him Harrison Ford, Kevin Costner, George Clooney, Brad Pitt *some*times. How'd I do?"

"Pretty good," I said. Did I really prefer older men?

"You know," Betina said, "I didn't think about this at the time, but when Woodley asked me what actors August likes, I listed off the same guys you like. Isn't that funny?"

I didn't answer because I was busy exchanging a "Did you hear what I heard?" look with Nellie. She put down the last bite of her sandwich.

"So August was interested in older guys?" Nellie asked Betina.

"Hmmm." Betina thought hard about that one. "She liked older guys in movies. I never saw her go out with an older guy."

"Betina, you've said you rarely saw her go out with younger guys," Nellie observed.

"Say," Betina almost whispered, as if someone might overhear, "Do you think she didn't go out with young guys because she has a thing for older men?"

"It's a theory," Nellie said, giving me the side eye.

I looked at my watch. Ten minutes of lunch time was about enough for today.

"Nellie," I said, "I have an inventory question for you." I headed for the back room with Nellie right behind me.

"Harrison Ford's a little old for you, isn't he?"

"Just think how old he is for August," I said. "Which doesn't necessarily mean that the slut dress at Connor's is hers."

"Lingerie?" Nellie said.

"Let's agree to call it slutty lingerie."

"Don't be a prude."

"Do you think I'm a prude to think that August is a slut if she has a thing with Connor? Am I just jealous?"

"Both?" Nellie said. "It's OK with me if August has a *thing* with any male older than eighteen. Except one, obviously."

"Now who's jealous?"

"Oh, come on," Nellie said. "Rudy is my lawfully wedded boat anchor. You never had *any* sign from Connor that he was *your* thing."

"He let me look after his dog," I said defensively.

"The basis of a true and lasting relationship," she said.

"Look, the important question is, ah, what?" I said. "What is the important question? Oh yeah! Does this have anything to do with Annie's murder?"

"Here's a question: Was August angry that Annie outed her?" Nellie asked.

"Because," I said, "whether we think August is a slut doesn't matter. It's what August wants us to think that matters."

"Because," Nellie said, "August clearly hid her older-man thing from everybody."

"If she actually does have an older-man thing," I noted.

"Are we just making this up?"

I sighed. "Let's go cut some hair."

"Actually," Nellie said, "I was going to ask if I could take the afternoon off to fetch my two boys from the Tickfaw campground. Having them there by themselves kept me awake most of last night, and I've been frazzled all morning. I've only got two clients this afternoon. Could you cover for me?"

I readily agreed. I only had two clients myself, and the idea of the boys camping by themselves in the swamp kept me awake, too.

The afternoon got under way at the same sedate pace as the morning. But as the earlier overcast had gradually broken up and the sky looked less like rain, more people came to hang out in our café area. Someone asked if we were about to start offering Botox injections — "news" of our morning Botox discussion had got out — and an afternoon Botox discussion was well underway. The afternoon crept by until Connor showed up.

I wasn't happy to see him and I'm sure the look on my face said, *What are you doing here?* What I said out loud was, "Do you need a trim?"

He answered the look on my face. "You asked me to come look at a rack that's broken?"

"Ah," I said, with a tone of voice that must have communicated, *Why couldn't you have forgotten and never darkened my door again?*

I showed him the foot of the rack Betina noticed was broken. We had propped up that corner with a brick. I was thinking now that I liked the look of the brick. Gave it a shabby chic, well mainly shabby look. I could definitely live with the brick if Connor would just go away.

He took a quick look and told me that the rack was wrought iron, which I already knew, and that welding wrought iron wasn't a good idea, especially in a high-stress area.

"Like my salon?" I asked, puzzled.

"What?" he asked, equally puzzled.

"My salon is a high-stress area?"

"Ehm, no, no, the foot of the rack has a lot of stress on it because of the weight. A weld won't hold."

I thanked him for taking a look and said, "See you later," as I walked back to my station.

"I could forge a new part," he said then, "and fasten it on with stove bolts, just like the original."

I walked back toward the rack trying to think of a way to say *Please go away* with a look on my face, or my tone of voice, or should I just say it out loud? Why was this man being so exasperating?

When I got close to him he surprised me by leaning down and saying quietly in the Irish accent I used to find so charming, "I know what you must think of me. I'm sorry."

I looked into his eyes and saw just about the deepest sadness I'd ever seen, loss pulled out from under loss. He quickly bowed his head and said he'd be going.

"Conner?" I said. "Go ahead and forge a new part."

He nodded quickly and was gone. My heart felt like it'd been whacked around like a raquet ball. Maybe staying single and forgoing all men was what I needed. And men say women are difficult. Pshaw!

A little before five Nellie came bursting in the front door, all out of breath.

"That was fast," I started saying before I switched quickly to "Is something wrong with the boys?"

"No," she gasped. "They're fine. But they discovered something that will make your head spin." She leaned against the front counter. Everyone in the salon stopped what they were doing. "On the Internet they found pictures of August Anderson in several different outfits that were *very* revealing."

"Slut dresses?" I asked.

"Some people might call them that," she replied with a wry smile. "The thing is, they were expensive-looking dresses, not cheap trash. And that's not the most amazing part."

The jaws of most people in the salon had already dropped because the cat was out of the bag that the SLUT painted on August's windshield just might be accurate. Nellie proceeded to dump out another cat...this one more like a cougar.

"Some of the photos show a man helping August out of the outfits and, as my oldest son put it, 'doing the nasty.'"

And then Nellie let out the final screeching banshee. "The man having sex with August was Burl Botowski."

Now *every* jaw in the place dropped because Burl Botowski was more than twice August's age, and more importantly, because Betina was at that moment doing the highlights in Hildebrand Botowski's hair. Strands of hair all over Hildebrand's head were wrapped in foil.

Every slack-jawed person in the salon looked at Hildebrand except Betina, who looked at Nellie, who looked at Betina. Nellie was mystified why everyone was not looking at her, until she recognized Hildebrand, who had not moved, aside from her jaw. It dawned on Nellie that letting that last cat out of the bag in front of Hildebrand might have consequences.

With the pink salon smock billowing around her, foil-wrapped hair sticking out all over her head, and a look of murderous intent on her face, Hildebrand exploded out of the chair and through the front door. Nellie and I bounded after her, followed closely by everyone else in the salon.

We all knew where Hildebrand was going and what she was going to do when she got there. For an older and slightly rotund woman, she could sure move when a fire was lit under her tail.

She blew down Clifton Street and into Botowski Hardware. As we came in the door, we heard the roar of a Stihl MS250c chainsaw cranking up. Hildebrand favored that model because of its easy-start feature. Two or three gentle tugs on the starting cord, and you're ready to dismember your philandering husband.

I don't think Hildebrand intended to dismember Burl. On the other hand, her intentions probably weren't clearly formed in her mind even when she revved the Stihl and ran with it full tilt toward the back of the store where she knew he'd be.

Burl had come out of the back office when he heard the chainsaw start, since he didn't trust their only employee (a teenager named Douglas) to demo a chainsaw properly. When Burl saw Hildegard in the pink smock sprinting toward him with the Stihl, he ducked back into the office and slammed the door. Douglas was standing in the paint section looking on with a gaping mouth.

Hildegard had already engaged the saw's chain before she passed the hand tool section. She put the tip of the 16-inch bar against the office door, and the saw bounced around for a while before the chain caught purchase and began to rip. She cut a clean oval out of the door that was about her size. I can only imagine what this must have been like from Burl's point of view, trapped inside the office.

It's possible that cutting a Hildegard-sized hole in the hardwood door appeased her anger a little, or it could be that her exertions had tired her out. Or, as I say, she never intended to dismember Burl....I think.

Whatever the reason, Hildegard paused before going through the hole she'd made, and we saw a stream of red hit her face. Burl had pepper-sprayed her. Not the best idea.

This was not necessarily a good defensive play because Hildegard immediately plunged through the opening in the door with the chainsaw, completely enraged and blind as a bat. We could hear the chainsaw biting through a lot of stuff and feared that some of it might be Burl.

With a hunch that Hildegard wasn't going to last long with pepper in her eyes, Nellie asked Douglas if the store had an eye-wash station. Of course, they didn't, but Nellie remembered the Gatorade in a cooler by the register. She threw a couple of bottles to me, grabbed a couple more, and we headed toward the back of the store.

By that time Hildegard had thrown down the chainsaw with a thud. When we got through the hole in the door, expecting to see blood everywhere, Hildegard was standing with her face covered in red pepper spray and her hair flailing out all over her head in strips of aluminum foil. She was screaming in anger and frustration. Also pain.

As we doused Hildegard's face with Gatorade, Burl made his getaway through the hole in the door. He didn't seem to be missing any parts as far as I could see. Fortunately, Hildegard couldn't see him. Nellie told Hildegard sensibly that she needed to calm down and come back to the salon right now or her highlights would be ruined. Now that's how you calm down a vengeful woman...tell her her hair will be fried to a frizzle if she doesn't cooperate.

Back in the salon, Nellie rinsed off her thoroughly at the hair-washing station. Hildegard told us that she'd mainly been angry because she had realized why money must have constantly been missing from the hardware store's accounts. "It won't break my heart that he bonked that tart," she said. "But he better stop messing with my money." Ahhh, true love.

Chapter 14

Nellie invited me to my house for dinner. She said she would have invited me to her house, but she had left her boy Dale with Mrs. Chabert, who lived a couple of houses away from me. As long as she was picking up Dale so close, we might as well eat at my house. All very logical.

Dinner consisted of tacos I picked up from the Paramabets on my way home. We parked Dale in front of the TV with his taco so we could talk in the kitchen.

Nellie's tale of the August pictures was even stranger than what she had revealed in the salon. When she arrived at the boys' tent in the campground, they were wearing ear buds and sitting in front of their laptop computers. A slide show was clicking by on each of the laptops.

She quickly realized that some of the slide show photos looked like porn. She was about to swat Aubrey's head when she recognized August in the photos. And then she recognized Burl. Then she swatted Aubrey's head.

The boys hadn't simply found this material deposited on the Internet somewhere. They had got it off the state of Louisiana's law enforcement network.

The father of the nice family from Shreveport the boys had befriended turned out to be an ex-cop who was disgruntled with his former superiors. He'd showed the boys how to get into the state's network, which was great fun as well as useful. The boys regularly checked the law enforcement database to see if anyone was investigating the moonshining operation.

On one of their research expeditions into the database, they noticed the name of Annie Simmerson. They knew that Annie was a witch because she'd been mean to them at their doctor appointments. They reminded Nellie they'd complained at the time about Annie poking them and banging them with things for no reason. Nellie had waved off their complaints as typical kid discomfort with medical procedures.

The boys did a search for everything on the law enforcement network relating to Annie and found that a forensics team had attached Annie's laptop to their network so that everyone on the team could work on hacking into it. Now the boys could try hacking it, too, and because they had poked around in Annie's purse when she wasn't looking in the doctor's office, they had a starting point for guessing her password. That's how they found the photos.

"You're saying they found the August porn on Annie's computer?" I asked.

"That's right," she said, putting down her taco. "So when I told the story in the salon this afternoon, I couldn't mention the most amazing fact of all. Annie had those photos. It looked like she had somehow taken them secretly, but I wonder if she kept it a secret from Burl."

"You think she was blackmailing him?"

"If she wasn't blackmailing him, what *was* she doing with the photos?" Nellie said.

"Maybe she just liked watching," I said doubtfully. I chewed on my taco for a moment. "She could have been blackmailing August, but August didn't have money. Did she?"

"She did if she got money from Burl," Nellie said. "But surely Annie would go directly to the source. Unless."

"Unless she was just interested in tormenting August," I said, catching Nellie's drift.

"Whatever's going on, I've got a little problem now that I've gone public with some of this info, and Hildegard has carved up the hardware store. Investigator James Woodley will want to know how I came by this info. I left the two boys in the campground so they wouldn't be handy for him to interrogate."

"That was smart," I said. "Even if it makes the mom uncomfortable. Can't have him finding out about the moonshining before the new still is licensed."

"Mom will just have to have faith that her boys can take care of themselves."

"As they obviously can," I observed hopefully.

"In any case, we need to figure out what we can tell Woodley," Nellie said. "What I can tell Woodley, I mean."

I got up and threw our empty taco containers in the trash. "You could play dumb," I suggested.

"It's an approach that plays to my strengths," Nellie said. "It's also a lie on the face of it. I demonstrated that I do know something in front of a salon full of people. And it's something that the police don't know about."

"And since they don't know about it, you were just passing on gossip."

"Ah, good point. I was thinking I had revealed *facts*."

"How about some ice cream?" I asked. "Choc chip?"

She held out her arm. I twisted it. "If you insist," she said.

"The thing is," she said, "the police will get into Annie's laptop at some point, and they'll wonder how I knew what was in it before they did. I would really prefer not to be mixed up in a murder case, you know?"

I put a bowl of ice cream in front of her. "Speaking of which," I said, "there's a murderer out there. None of us are safe until they catch this person. We can't hold back information that could be important."

I took a bowl of ice cream out to Dale and then sat down at the table with my own.

"How about if I get my boys to spread the August-and-Burl photos around the Internet?" Nellie said. "I told people in the salon that that's where the boys found the photos."

"That's cruel to August, isn't it?"

"Yeah," Nellie admitted. "It's one thing to tell people that a girl is a slut and another thing to give photographic proof." Nellie studied the taste of her ice cream for a moment. "She looked hot, by the way."

"Nellie!"

"I'm just saying."

"The other issue," I said, "is that the police don't know that Annie had the photos. They need to know that."

"August is already a suspect," Nellie said. "This makes her more of a suspect. And now Burl is added to the suspect list."

"But only if the police know all this."

"How about if my boys give Annie's password to the police?" Nellie proposed. "Help those guys out a little?"

"That would work, if they can do it without blowing their cover."

"Beyond me," Nellie said. "The other problem with any plan involving the boys is that I'll have to drive back over to the Tickfaw."

"And you still need a cover story to tell Woodley."

"I could drive over to the Tickfaw and stay there until the heat blows over," Nellie said. "Is that the right way to say it?"

"Something like that," I said, "And it's a good plan if you want to look more suspicious." I put our empty ice cream bowls in the sink. "Hey, how about all of the above?" I said.

"All of us go stay on the Tickfaw?"

"Yeah, get away from here. That sounds nice," I said. "But what I mean is, spread some of the less revealing photos around the Internet and give the police the password."

"OK," Nellie said. "That would give the police the evidence they need, and it would mean I *could* have seen the photos on the Internet." She frowned. "If only I had a way to see anything on the Internet. How does that work?"

"I've never been on the Internet," I said.

"Me neither."

"But Woodley doesn't know that. You just need a good story about how you've been on the Internet. You tell him where you saw the photos. He goes and finds them there. Everything looks good."

"Actually, I just remembered that my brother told me about those photos. He knew August before he moved to Houston. I think he'd be willing to confess that he trolls the Internet for porn."

Sounded like a plan to me. I offered to drive to the Tickfaw to spare Nellie another trip, but she figured she might as well take the opportunity to see the boys again. We agreed that I'd keep Dale overnight and drop him off at Mrs. Chabert's on my way to the salon in the morning.

Before Nellie left, she had a moment of doubt about what she was planning.

"Isn't it a felony to lie to a state investigator?" she wondered.

"Probably," I shrugged. "What's your point?"

She admitted that it was just one more thing. We tallied up her family's felony count: moonshining for Rudy and his granddaddy; aiding and abetting for Nellie and the boys; hacking into the state law enforcement network; interfering with a murder investigation; and now lying to a state investigator.

"What's the old saying?" I asked. "Hang for a penny, hang for a pound?"

"Thanks, that's making me feel better," she said. "And I don't even know what that means."

"I think it means they'll nail you for part of a Monty, so you might as well go for the full Monty."

"That seems to be what August went for."

***

I was relieved to see Nellie coming in the front door of the salon the next morning, safe and sound. Other people were already there, so she gave me a casual thumbs up and went to work on Dolores Pettigrew's perm. The café area filled up early as people came in wanting to talk about August and Burl.

We expected to see Investigator Woodley first thing. I don't know why, since he always looked as if he'd just woken up if we saw him early in the afternoon. Nellie was anxious to get the interview over, so the wait was wearing on her.

When we finally did see Woodley around 11:30, it didn't go the way we expected. He threw open the front door, came halfway in, and shouted, "Nellie Phlint?"

Caught by surprise, Nellie looked at him and raised her hand slowly.

"Come with me," he barked.

"Am I under arrest?" she asked.

Dolores Pettigrew, who was in the café area showing off her new perm, said, "Remember you get one phone call."

Woodley looked exasperated. "Come right now!" he insisted. "It's your son."

Had they tracked down Aubrey for hacking into the law enforcement network? Egads!

Pete didn't have a client at the moment, so I motioned to him to take over the cut I was mostly done with and hurried out the door. I expected to see Woodley bundling Nellie into his white Ford Expedition, but they had gone past the Expedition and were hustling down Clifton Street in the direction of Botowski Hardware. I hustled after them.

To my surprise, they ran past the hardware store and turned left at the corner. As I passed the hardware store, I noticed Burl in the chainsaw section, fastening down a McCulloch model with a wire cable.

I rounded the corner in time to see Nellie and Woodley dash into Dr. Cason's office. It dawned on me that this might have something to do with Dale. But why was Woodley involved?

When I got into the doctor's office, Woodley was standing in the waiting room shaking his head. The door to the back was open. I heard Dale telling his mother loudly that he was all right. Woodley motioned me out the door and came out with me.

"What's wrong with Dale?" I demanded.

"He's been shot. A little," Woodley explained. I turned to go back in the doctor's office.

He stopped me.

"Don't worry," he reassured me. "As Dale said, he's all right." Woodley let out a deep breath. "Could easily have been much worse."

"What happened?" I asked. "You didn't shoot him?"

"Me?" he asked incredulously. "Why would you even think that?"

"Why else would you be involved?"

"Because I saw it happen. I was driving down Tennessee Street to come to your shop and saw three children playing — near your house, as a matter of fact. I noticed that they were playing with a very realistic-looking rifle, and then it went off."

Woodley turned and put his hands on the brick building. He was trembling. Without thinking, I put my hand on his arm. He looked at me. "I see a lot of things in this line of work," he said. "Seeing something bad happen to a child..." He left the thought unfinished.

"Let's walk a little," I suggested.

He shook his head and straightened up. "I've got to get the rifle to the forensics lab in Baton Rouge."

"I'll walk you back to your car," I said. "Where did the kids get the rifle?"

"They found it in a ditch."

Those kids had been playing a couple of doors down from my house. "You think it's the gun that killed Annie."

"Looks to me like it'd been in that ditch a week, max. We'll see what forensics thinks."

We said our goodbyes and I watched him drive away. Then I walked quickly back to Dr. Cason's office.

The bullet had grazed Dale's shoulder and forehead, but his biggest injury was powder burns because the gun had gone off so close to him. His hearing seemed to be OK, though his ears were ringing badly. Dr. Cason gauzed him up so that he looked like a mummy, which Dale didn't think was funny.

After Nellie got the mummy buckled into the SUV, she told me that when she had arrived at the Tickfaw campground the night before, she found her boys hard at work messing with Annie's laptop. They told Nellie that night time was best for what they were doing because they had the laptop all to themselves. Aubrey said, "The guys in the state forensics lab are not putting in any overtime."

The boys told her they could secretly help the forensics team by adding passwords to their database. And they could easily spread some of the photos of August and Burl around the Internet. "Yay," was Nellie's comment on that activity.

Nellie insisted on helping them pick photos that were relatively mild, which meant paging through the collection. "Looking through porn with your small boys is odd," she said. "Potentially educational when we have the time to chat about it."

The boys also told her they had decrypted more photos from Annie's laptop.

"They were in a crypt?" I asked.

"Spooky, isn't it?" Nellie said. "Want to guess who was in these photos?"

"Connor?" I guessed. "And August?"

"Reasonable guess," she said. "Try Dr. Cason."

"Dr. Cason with August?" That wasn't reasonable. Doctors were supposed to be above this, weren't they?

"Some of the photos were taken in the examining room where he was treating Dale," Nellie said. "Once I realized that Dale would be OK, I looked around and recognized a landscape print on the wall. It was all I could do to keep from saying something about playing doctor in that room."

"August is definitely a slut," I observed, thinking out loud. "Which is unbelievable, so I'm also starting to believe the more unbelievable thing: that August is a murderer."

"At this point, I can believe just about anything."

The mummy was starting to raise a ruckus in the SUV. Nellie told him to hang on. She opened the driver's side door and stopped.

"The problem is," she said, "once we start believing unbelievable things, where do we stop?"

Chapter 15

When I got back to the salon, I told people that Dale had accidentally been shot with the murder weapon. Or probably the murder weapon. Everyone wondered why the police hadn't found the rifle before the children did.

"Aren't they supposed to search for something like that?" Dolores Pettigrew asked.

"Looks like the police should be hiring children to do the searching," some wag commented.

They should also be hiring children to hack into laptops. That thought reminded me that the excitement with the rifle had kept Woodley from interviewing Nellie about the August/Burl photos. The forensics people should have those photos when Woodley showed up with the rifle, so Nellie might be off the hook.

Now if Woodley could identify the murderer based on all that, we could all go back to whatever it was we were doing before this mess started. I had a vague recollection that everything was nice and unexciting.

The odd thing was, so many people had been living lives that were different from what we thought. Rudy and his granddaddy were moonshining. Burl, Dr. Cason, and possibly Connor were moonlighting with August. Annie was tormenting half the population.

In a small town, everybody is supposed to know everybody's business. Apparently, that hadn't been true in Knockemstiff for a long time. At the rate we were going, though, everybody was going to end up knowing way too much about everybody's business.

In the salon, we talked about everybody's business. The highlight of this afternoon was when Angela Ladecky brought in blueberry mini-muffins to sell in our café area. Just after that a light drizzle of rain set in, and everything seemed subdued and quiet. The light of the day faded early.

Tonight was my usual night to have dinner with friends at the Bacon Up. As I closed up the salon, I thought about the fact it had been a week since I'd found Annie dead on the side of the road after my last dinner at the Bacon Up. The thought didn't inspire a craving for bacon. I'd be happy with yogurt and a Godzilla movie.

Just when I had decided to walk around to the Bacon Up and let them know I was cashing out early tonight, my friend Eva saw me and waved. I tried to tell her that I was skipping the bacon this time, but she said, "What? My hearing aide batteries are about dead." (She doesn't have hearing aides.) Then she grabbed my arm and led me to the Bacon Up in the drizzling rain.

A couple of hours later I was walking back to where my car was parked, and doing pretty well since I'd only had one beer this time, when I saw a big, dark figure lurking in front of the salon. I was wondering what it was about bacon night that led to seeing scary things when I heard the figure call "Savannah?" in an Irish accent.

"Connor?" I said. "What are you doing out here?"

"Savannah, sorry to startle you. I brought the new part for your rack."

"Rack?" I said. "Now?"

I couldn't see how one beer could keep me from understanding how working on the rack at this hour made sense. I was pretty sure this did *not* make sense. "This doesn't make sense," I pointed out.

"Yeah, I know," he said. "I was going by the diner, and I saw you, and I was hoping we could talk."

"Talk?" I said. "Now?"

I don't think I'm an overly judgmental person. (If I did think that, I'd be overly judgmental, wouldn't I?) I figure people can pretty much behave however they want. If I don't care for someone's behavior, I'll spend my time with someone else. That's not a judgment; that's a preference. And when I make my preference, I'm impatient with people who insist that I mustn't misunderstand them. I want to say, *I'm sure you have perfectly good reasons for behaving like a dope; I don't care.* That does sound a bit judgmental. Oh well.

I was about to tell Connor that he could make an appointment to get his hair cut, and I would listen to him talk for half an hour, when he said "Please, Savannah" with such deep Irish anguish in his voice, it somehow reminded me that this wasn't only about my preference. This might have something to do with a murder.

"Damn!" I muttered under my breath. Good thing little Sarah wasn't around. I'd be setting a bad example.

I fished the tangle of keys out of my purse, and as I turned the key in the lock, it occurred to me to wonder if this was a safe move. Specifically: was Connor a murderer? Had Annie been jealous of Connor's *thing* with August and tried to blackmail him? Or had Annie just wanted to expose what was going on in a way that ruined August's relationship with Connor? Had that made this Irish poet angry enough to kill? Did he now intend to kill me because I knew too much?

It's amazing the number of thoughts you can have in the space of time it takes to turn a key. You can break out in a cold sweat just that fast, too.

It seemed a little late to run away. I pushed open the door and tried to think of something that might serve as a club that I could stand next to. The coat rack? Broom? How about something sharp?

Before I turned on the lights, I walked to my station, thinking I could grab my scissors in the dark and hide them behind me. I knew exactly where they were.

I was picking up the scissors when the lights came on. Connor had found the switch. He was looking at me, frowning, holding a cloth bag in his hand that was obviously heavy.

"Ah," he said, looking at the scissors in my hand. "You think I'm here to kill you." He sat in a chair in the café area and put the cloth bag down with a metallic plonk. "And why wouldn't you think that?"

"I don't know what to think about anything anymore," I said. "Everyone turns out to be different than they seemed a couple of weeks ago."

"I'm certainly different," he said. "But I'm not here to kill you."

"Would you like a cup of tea?" I asked automatically. If he wasn't going to kill me, I felt like I should be a good hostess.

He laughed. "Yes, that would be lovely."

I put down the scissors. He really didn't seem like a killer.

While I filled the electric kettle, Connor began to tell me why he had come. "It hurts that you think ill of me," he said, "I can chalk that up to my own folly. But after I'm gone, your thinking ill of August will hang like a millstone around my neck."

"You're going away?" I asked in surprise.

"It's for the best. I can't see how August can continue to live here, but in case she wants to, I'd like for you to understand her a little better."

"Well," I said, "I understand pretty well that she's your slut."

He winced. "Savannah, she's the opposite of that. She's like a flower child from the 1960s. She sees love as a form of play. She doesn't understand why other people take it so seriously. She just wants to revel in it."

"Why can't she 'revel in it' with boys her own age?"

"I think she figured out early on that boys her age were certainly willing to play at love, but they were mostly interested in their own fun and saw her as a play*thing*. She had the idea that love could be a complete communion of two people, a commingling of mind, body and spirit. I'm sure there are any number of 20-something boys in the world who have the same idea, but August didn't know any in Knockemstiff."

I handed him a cup of hot water with a teabag in it. "So you volunteered to commingle with her," I said.

"She approached me, Savannah. She heard me read at open mic several times and told me she liked my poetry." He dunked his teabag reflectively. "You'd be surprised how many women are attracted by poetry." He gave me a little of his sly Irish smile.

I dunked my own teabag reflectively, thinking how nice it would be if they made teabags that would brew a cup of beer instead of tea. I'm not much of a tea drinker, especially when I'm listening to a tale that cries out for a beer.

I sighed. "August found your poetry irresistible. One thing led to another. And the 'nother' looked very much like August being your slut, only it wasn't that."

"Exactly!" Connor said as if I'd just clarified everything. He took the teabag out of his cup and looked around. I held out a trash can for it and added my own teabag to the can.

"August wanted to create a separate space for love play, where two people could go into a room and express themselves with a sense of joy. When we came out of that room, we left it behind. It wasn't about obligations or expectations, except that we committed to keep it private and never be hurtful. It was play."

"What a peculiar idea," I said, "that you could go into a room, do whatever you pleased, and when you came out, all the consequences would stay in that room. Connor, forgive me, but this sounds like a male fantasy."

"It *was* a male fantasy. And what I'm telling you is that it was also a female fantasy. I wanted to bring August with me, so she could tell you herself, but she still isn't entirely well."

"August is ill?"

"She has had a medical problem, thanks to Annie Simmerson."

He stood up and started pacing and waving his hands. "When August went to Dr. Cason to get her prescription for birth control pills renewed, Annie added a second prescription for an antibiotic that's closely related to one that August is allergic to. August didn't think anything about it. She took both prescriptions to the pharmacy in Paudy, where they don't have a record of her allergies, and she started taking the antibiotic. When she had a reaction, she still didn't think about it and kept taking the pills. She ended up with a severe reaction and other problems, I think."

He stopped pacing and looked at me. "That Annie was a devil."

"So I've heard," I said. "Is August going to be all right?"

"Dr. Cason says so. He gave August something to stop the allergic reaction from closing off her windpipe. That was last Wednesday. Mostly after that it was just a matter of time."

He took a sip of his tea, and then put down the cup and picked up the cloth bag. He took it over to the metal rack.

"Someone mentioned they saw you and Dr. Cason rushing away from his office last Wednesday, each of you with a sheaf of papers."

"That was after I figured out that Annie had caused August's problem, and I remembered what happened with Mrs. Toler when Annie got her to cut her insulin." He sat down on the floor and pulled tools out of his bag.

"How did you know about that?" I asked.

"I'm the one who found Mrs. Toler almost dead. I used to visit her from time to time. She didn't get out, and she sometimes needed something fixed, or mostly just someone to listen for a few minutes. Anyway, I told Dr. Cason that we had to search for other cases of Annie mischief. We found lots. Some of them we couldn't get on the phone right away, so we divvied them up and went out to make sure people were OK."

"Were people OK?"

"A few were in a very bad way. One old guy is still in critical condition." He was taking the bolts out of the old part. "I don't know why Dr. Cason didn't check for these problems sooner, unless Annie had some leverage on him."

Did Connor not know that Dr. Cason had a thing with August? Or did he not know that Annie knew? Maybe Connor just didn't want me to know.

He was already bolting the new part on the rack.

"Connor, how did you make that new part without taking measurements?"

"I wondered if you would notice that. This rack was made by the smith who owned my forge before me. When I bought the forge, he left behind an identical rack in the workshop. He was meticulous in his specs. I knew that if I made a part that fit my rack, it would fit the twin that you have here. And there it is."

He pulled the brick out from underneath the rack, put his tools back in the cloth bag, and walked out of the salon without another word.

Chapter 16

The drizzle was still coming down on Wednesday morning. Betina came in all in a tizzy about seeing someone prowling around her cottage after midnight.

"It wasn't exactly strolling weather," she said, "so he was obviously up to something. I couldn't sleep for the rest of the night."

"Wasn't it awfully dark with the rain and all?" I asked. "How could you tell it was a he?" I was wondering if Connor had skulked all over town after he left the salon.

"My neighbors left one of their outside lights on," Betina said. "I could see it was a man all right, a big man. He stood outside and looked directly at my window for a long time, at least five minutes."

"It was probably a zombie out looking for brains to eat," said Nellie, "and finding the pickings pretty slim."

Betina would typically have replied with "Ha, ha," or something similarly penetrating. She thought that she was a smart cookie. In fact, Betina had no self-esteem issues whatsoever.

"Everyone knows that zombies walk with that stooped-over shuffle," she said. "This man walked completely upright."

"Was there a bad smell in the air?" Pete asked. "Like rotten meat?"

Betina paused in shampooing Mrs. Larson and tried to put her nose back at the scene. "No. It was mostly just damp smelling. Maybe a little moldy, but that's a problem I have on that side of the cottage." She resumed shampooing Mrs. Larson. "I need to take everything out of my bedroom and wipe the walls down with bleach. I've heard that that will cure mold and mildew problems."

"Was there an article in *Nylon* about that?" Pete asked.

"Um, I don't remember where I heard that mildew thing," Betina said. "But I did see an article in *Nylon* about using bleach to customize jeans. You paint the bleach on the denim to make designs. Isn't that clever?"

"I've actually done that myself," Nellie said, "although I'm unclear on the distinction between customizing and ruining."

"I can't remember the last time I saw you in jeans, Betina," Pete said. "Are you thinking of branching out with your wardrobe?"

Betina seemed surprised by the question. "You think I'd look good in jeans?" She cocked her body sideways and put her hand on her hip like a runway model. She was wearing one of her skimpiest sun dresses despite the drizzle outside.

"That's a cute dress," Pete said.

"Thank you," Betina said brightly. She was massaging conditioner into Mrs. Larson's hair.

"Do you have a date tonight with a hot, studly guy?" he asked.

"She's hoping Woodley will pay us a visit," Nellie said.

Pete looked disappointed. He didn't find Woodley hot or studly.

"If Investigator Woodley does visit," Betina replied tartly, rinsing out the conditioner. "I'm going to ask him for some protection against prowlers, which are probably murderers. I'm terrified half to death."

"Did you call the police last night?" Mrs. Larson asked.

"I did call the police," Betina said. "You know it's hard to call the police when you're trying to stay really quiet. Those noises that come out of the phone when you press the buttons? They're tipping off the murderer that you're in there dialing the cops, and he's going to make his move. I'm surprised I'm not dead."

"What happened with the police, Betina?" Mrs. Larson asked as she walked to Betina's station with a towel around her head.

"Well, I woke Digby up. I had to whisper to keep from alerting the murderer, and Digby kept saying 'What? What?' and I'm whispering 'Digby, it's me' and he said, 'Is this some kind of telemarketing thing," and I said real loud, 'Digby! I'm being stalked by a murderer.' I thought then I was a goner. I took the phone into the bathroom and crouched in the tub. You know how they tell you to get in the tub because it's safer?"

"I remember when Eileen Brenner saved her life by getting in the tub during that hurricane," Pete said. "Hurricane Bosco? Something like that. Her whole house was blown away, and there she was safe in the tub."

"You'd think the tub would fill up with rain during a hurricane," Betina said.

"Yeah, they should tell you to make sure the drain's open," Pete said.

Lord have mercy!

"Did Digby come?" Mrs. Larson asked.

"He certainly did not want to," Betina said. "I told him I was crouched in the tub, knowing that any moment the murderer was going to bust in and kill me, and Digby asks me if this prowler is one of the guys I've rejected wanting attention. I told him I would never date a guy who slouched around in the dark in a trench coat."

"I thought you said this guy was walking completely upright," Nellie protested.

"Well, he was slouched a little, all right?" Betina said. "He wasn't lurking around with perfect posture or anything."

"So his posture was maybe halfway between a zombie and a date?" Pete asked.

"What did Digby do?" Mrs. Larson insisted.

"Digby said that if the prowler tried to come in the house, I should shoot him," Betina said.

"What?" said Mrs. Larson with alarm.

"Yes!" Betina said. "I said, 'Digby, you nimnal, how can I shoot him if I don't have a gun?' He said, 'How could you not have a gun? You're the only person in this town who doesn't have a gun.' I said to him, 'I would run right over to Botowski's and buy a gun, except it's the middle of the night and there's a murderer right outside my door.'"

Betina shook her head with exasperation. "Honestly!" she said.

"So did Digby come?" asked Mrs. Larson.

"He said, 'Stay right where you are. I'll bring you a gun.' I said, 'Digby, how will I know it's you and not the murderer?' He said he would knock three times then pause then two times more. 'OK,' I said."

"He brought you a gun, really?" asked Mrs. Larson.

"He did, a big gun, one of those shotguns with *two* barrels. He showed me how to pull the triggers. I said, 'Digby, there's only one murderer.' He said that I might miss with the first barrel. I told him that if the murderer tried to come in my house, I would not miss."

Now Nellie was looking slightly alarmed. She had a lot of experience worrying about guns.

"Did Digby show you how to work the safety?" she asked.

"Safety?" Betina asked.

"The little lever on the top of the barrel," Nellie said.

Betina had no knowledge of safety theory or practice. Nellie said she would show her how to use it at lunch time.

Pete and Nellie made light of Betina's fear of the prowler, but it wasn't funny to me after the encounter with Connor the night before. I'd been reminded that a murderer was still on the loose, and it could be anyone. We still weren't sure why Annie had been killed, so who might be next?

No one joked when Dolores Pettigrew came in and told us with uncharacteristic brevity that she had seen a prowler in the middle of the night. Normally, Pete and Nellie would have had a lot of fun at Dolores' expense over something like this, but Dolores was so seriously afraid, even they didn't find it amusing.

Dolores was close to tears. She told us that a man in a trench coat had walked back and forth outside her house for more than half an hour. At one point, he went to a shed in her side yard and tried to open the door. Dolores had been so afraid, she hadn't called the police for fear of making any noise.

When Betina heard all this, she exclaimed, "Dolores, you should get a shotgun. That's what I did."

"I have a shotgun," Dolores said. "Goodness me, I would have been twice as afraid if I wasn't armed."

While everyone else talked about the murderer lurking in our midst, I distracted myself by thinking about Connor. It wasn't a comforting distraction. Why had he been so intent on getting me to understand August? Did he think I would help restore August's reputation? If it came out that she was playing her "game" with Dr. Cason as well as Burl Botowski and Connor, the vast majority of people in Knockemstiff would be unwilling to think of her as anything but a slut. Denise Cason and Hildegard Botowski would be most unwilling of all.

What about the flower child idea? By all reports, the 1960s hadn't arrived in Knockemstiff by the end of the 1970s, so everybody gave up on the peace-and-love concept without ever knowing what it was about. I remember when my daddy would notice some act of intolerance or abuse of power, he would sometimes say that he'd be happy if Knockemstiff just made it out of the 19th century in his lifetime. I believe we did.

These days, hardly anybody in Knockemstiff had any interest in hating anybody else. That didn't mean that the '60s had arrived. Where had August gotten this flower child idea?

By the time our late lunch time rolled around, the whole salon was in an uproar about the prowler, the two people who had seen "him" were not entirely sure anymore that it couldn't have been a woman, and I was expecting that they were about to accuse one another of being murderers. Despite the drizzle, I had to get out.

I thought I'd go to the Bacon Up for a BLT, but when I got there, I saw Woodley in a booth by the window. I put my head down and kept walking. He rapped on the glass with a ring on his right hand as I went by. I couldn't help but look, and he beckoned me in. Why couldn't I have stayed in the salon?

He was standing by the booth when I came in. "Please join me," he said, gesturing. "I've been meaning to talk to you."

I took off my raincoat and hung it on the coat rack. Margie, the waitress, jerked her thumb toward Woodley and gave me a throat slitting gesture with a questioning look. I reluctantly shook my head, no.

"I don't think I can tell you any more than I have," I said to him as I sat down.

He looked at me with mild amusement, as though he was surprised to hear that I thought he would believe that I had told him everything. "Let me just ask you," he said, "if you know where August Anderson is."

"I don't," I said. "You mean, you don't know where she is?"

Margie set a cup in front of me and poured coffee into it.

"Your powers of deduction are spot on," he said. "Let me tell you why I want to know. What if she has also been murdered?"

"No!" Margie and I said simultaneously.

Woodley glared at her. She raised the caffeinated and decaffeinated pots in a gesture of "sorry" and went back to the kitchen.

"Why do you think that?" I asked.

"I haven't been able to find anyone who's seen her since Monday of last week. I haven't found any trace of her. She's vanished."

"So she's either murdered or a murderer who's gotten away," I concluded.

He shrugged.

"Did you find her deer rifle when you searched her house?" I asked.

"How did you know...?" he started. "Ah. Got me. I did search her house, and I did not find the rifle, because..."

He looked at me expectantly over his bacon and eggs.

"It was in a ditch, where some kids found it," I concluded.

"Bingo," he said. "Forensics says it's 90% certain that the bullet that killed Annie was fired from that rifle. We traced the rifle back to a gun shop in Stanleyville. They sold it to an Ellis Anderson eight years ago."

"August's uncle," I said. "She used to go hunting with him."

"OK, thank you," he said. "Saved us a bit of work."

Marge set a BLT in front of me and retreated. I launched into it, thankful that Margie knew what I needed and that one good thing was happening to me today. Hello, bacon.

"I should probably talk to Chief Tanner about this," I said after chewing for a while. "A couple of people have mentioned in the salon that they saw a prowler last night. They're afraid that it might be the murderer."

"Did they give a description?" he asked.

"Doesn't sound like August," I said. "Betina says the prowler was a man who was slouching *slightly.* Therefore not a zombie."

He looked puzzled. "Zombies don't slouch?"

"Zombies *do* slouch," I explained. "A lot. Also shuffle." I chewed another bite of BLT. "Aren't you people on top of the zombie thing?"

"Some nights I feel like I know a lot about zombies," he said.

That's when I noticed the trench coat he was wearing. "Betina and the other woman said the prowler was wearing a trench coat."

"Ah," he said. "Definitely *was* a zombie. Zombie named Woodley."

"They were seriously afraid," I said. "Didn't sleep. Officer Digby brought Betina a double-barrel shotgun so she could protect herself."

"You're kidding," he said.

"Don't go near her house again, that's my advice."

"I don't even know where she lives," he said. "But I'll go around to the salon and apologize for frightening her. Maybe she'll give the shotgun back to officer Digby?"

"The horse is out of the barn there," I said. "Nellie is giving Betina a quick course on firearm safety right about now. Maybe that will help. The only real solution will be you catching the murderer."

But he wasn't listening because he'd spotted the Bald Eagle passing by. He rapped on the window with his ring, and the Eagle came in. He and I exchanged heys. Woodley asked if he'd join us. "I've been meaning to ask you something," Woodley said.

The Eagle sat down, and Margie poured him a cup of coffee.

I looked at my watch and said I needed to get back to the salon. The Eagle looked at the second half of my BLT and said that I was welcome to stay and finish my sandwich since I knew everything about him anyway.

"Does she know that you were having sex with August Anderson?" Woodley asked.

Sanders' smile evaporated. "I..." he said. It was the first time I'd ever seen him caught flat footed.

I reached across the table then and slapped Woodley hard on the shoulder.

"Hey!" he thundered. "You've just struck an officer of the law."

"I'm going to strike him a lot harder if he doesn't apologize to Sanders this instant," I hissed.

He blinked a couple of times, fast. He turned to the Eagle and said, "I am sorry, Mr. Bloomington. I used the situation unfairly. I regret my actions."

The Eagle stood up to go.

"Sanders, even if this got out — which it won't," I said quietly, with a sharp look at Woodley. "No one would think badly of you."

"Me?" he said with dismay. "It's not about me. What will people think of poor August for mixing it up with the Bald Eagle?" He stormed out of the diner.

"How dare you trick him like that," I said to Woodley.

"I apologized!" he said.

"Yeah, you regret your actions all right."

"OK, OK, that part was not perfectly on the level," he admitted. "What do you want? Do I play nice and let a killer go around loose?"

"You're playing dirty, and the killer is still going around loose," I pointed out. I stood up.

"I've had enough BLT," I said. "Come with me back to the salon, and you can apologize to Betina for ruining her night's sleep."

I put my coat on and turned up the collar. "You can pay," I told him. "And leave a big tip."

When we were out on the sidewalk, I asked him how he'd figured out that the Eagle was having a thing with August.

"What do you think I do all day?" he asked.

"Sleep?" I guessed.

"Savannah," he said, picking up a paper cup off the sidewalk. "Here I am awake, gathering important information." He tossed the cup in a trash bin.

"I regret my comment," I said, looking him over. "It does look like you got up at the crack of noon."

"Approximately," he said.

"By the way, why were you lurking around last night?"

"I wasn't lurking," he said. "Couldn't sleep. Helps me think if I walk. But the main reason is that I enjoy it. I have the town to myself. It's a pretty town. Somehow your little downtown survived when other little towns in Louisiana practically went to ruin."

He was right. Knockemstiff was something special. I loved this town. Would it continue to be lovable if everybody suspected everybody else of being a murderer?

Chapter 17

By Thursday morning, the drizzle had stopped. The sun rose through a few clouds in the east, and the day looked beautiful, a little cooler than our usual at this time of year. I wished I could walk to the salon.

I was like Woodley in that walking helped me think. I hadn't been doing much walking, so I felt as though I had a thousand unsorted letters from myself waiting to be opened and organized.

On any normal day before the murder, I would have had enough thinking to fill my day. What do you do when you've got all that thinking plus a murder's worth of thinking that needs doing? One thing you do is let normal things slide, so I was behind on paperwork at the salon — unopened mail, literally.

I went in early so I'd have the place to myself for a while. It gave me a chance to catch up on paperwork as well as sort through what had happened the previous day.

As I unlocked the front door of the salon, I felt as though a lot had happened, but only two facts seemed important: the rifle in the ditch belonged to August, and that rifle had killed Annie. I closed the front door behind me.

Oh, and August was missing. That might be the most important fact of all. Everything was pointing to August being the murderer.

And yet, as I walked over to the café area to make coffee, I was unable to believe that August could be a murderer. My disbelief was based on having known August her whole life, even if I didn't believe the flower-child story.

On the other hand, I'd also known Annie for most of her life, and I never knew the "real" Annie.

I filled the coffee pot at the hair-washing station. Did I know the real August? Obviously I hadn't really known her either. Having intimate relationships with four different men who were at least twice her age did not fit any portrait I would have drawn of that young woman. While the coffee perked, I wandered around the salon, straightening things, throwing things away.

Woodley wasn't swayed by knowing August. He must think she's the murderer. Yet he pointed out a second theory: that August could be another victim. I'd thought at the time he was trying to motivate me to tell him whatever I knew of August.

Did he think I knew where August was and that I was protecting her? If I did know where she was, I would know that she hadn't been murdered. That would leave theory one: she was the murderer.

I puttered around the salon wondering if Woodley had been fishing for confirmation of theory one when he talked to me. Or did he really think August could be another victim?

One thing I was sure of: Woodley wasn't sharing information with me randomly — except for the information about searching August's house that I'd tricked out of him. I smiled in amused self-appreciation. Sometimes I feel so clever I can hardly stand it.

I stopped puttering in front of the rack that Connor fixed. He said that August had a severe allergic reaction. When was that exactly? If it had been early last week, it was unlikely that August had been out shooting anybody.

I poured myself a cup of coffee and sat down. Did Woodley know about the allergic reaction? Dr. Cason must have told him about treating August, and Cason would have known where August was at that time. Or did Cason keep that to himself? He could be trying to protect August as well as his own reputation. He wouldn't want anyone to know that he'd let Annie harm patients for so long. Well, that wasn't under wraps any more.

I took my coffee into the back room and thought about how the previous day had finished in the salon. When I returned to the salon with Woodley after our late lunch, we found that Dolores was still there, afraid to go out. She said she'd only left her house that morning when the mailman arrived and she could walk to town with him. He had persuaded her to leave her shotgun at home.

Woodley apologized for frightening her and "attempting to violate the sanctity of her garden shed." A sudden downpour had prompted him to seek shelter. He explained that he'd been walking all around Knockemstiff, admiring our pretty little town. This was the best thing he could have said to Dolores, who was one of our most active and vocal town boosters — so active and so vocal that most of us wished she'd give it a rest now and then.

Woodley also apologized to Betina, who said she hadn't *really* been afraid. While Woodley was asking Nellie how Dale was doing, Betina turned around and undid two or three buttons at the neckline of her sun dress. Actually, it could have been four buttons.

Nellie had already told us that Dale was fine. In fact, she had dropped him off at Mrs. Chabert's as usual. Nellie said that she didn't feel like staying home with him, and she figured he wasn't likely to find another gun in the ditch.

After that, while Betina with her undone buttons was chatting up an amused Woodley, Nellie told me that she had gone to Betina's cottage at lunch time to look at the shotgun Digby had brought. The shotgun was not loaded. "It's a big old blunderbuss of a gun with plugs in the barrels so you couldn't load it if you wanted to," she said. "Betina can't hurt herself with it, so long as she doesn't drop it on her foot."

Nellie hadn't let on to Betina that the gun wouldn't fire. In fact, she had explained to Betina how the safety worked and that Betina should keep the gun broken until she wanted to use it. Betina observed that the term "broken" could not possibly be correct, and wondered why Nellie always acted as though Betina was a dim bulb. "I had trouble sounding sincere when I said that I didn't think she's a dim bulb," Nellie told me, "so this discussion was longer than it should have been."

In any case, Woodley had gone away forgiven by everyone but me, Dolores had gone home relieved, Betina had done up her buttons, and we all cut hair without further hubbub. I'd had a pleasant evening at home, not watching a Godzilla movie.

Now on Thursday morning I was sitting at my little desk in the back room thinking about everything except my paperwork. I picked up a stack of bills and got to work.

By the time the others came in, I had paid all the bills with money left over — always a nice feeling. Actually, the salon had pulled in more money than usual in the past week and a half, so Woodley was right. The murder had been good for business. That was not a nice feeling, but I could live with it.

We eased our way through the morning, talking about movies, current events and Botox, until Angela Ladecky brought in blueberry cupcakes for the café area. As icing on the cupcakes, she asked if we'd heard that Dr. Cason had had a fling with August.

Nellie looked at me and shrugged. I shrugged back. She and I hadn't spread around our knowledge of this fling, mostly because Nellie didn't want to have to explain how she'd come by that knowledge.

Nellie hadn't been back to visit her boys at the Tickfaw campground, so we didn't know if they had successfully shared the passwords to Annie's laptop with the police. Now I wondered if Nellie's boys had put some of the Dr. Cason photos on the Internet.

We found out more before the morning was out. Nadine Hines, Chief Tanner's part-time secretary, came in for a cup of coffee. When she heard everyone discussing Dr. Cason and August, she figured that cat was out of the bag so she could feel free to talk about it. (We found out later that Angela Ladecky had heard about this cat from Margie at the Bacon Up, who had heard it from Nadine — circular justification.)

"The state forensics lab succeeded in cracking Annie's laptop," Nadine said. "They must be very smart guys."

Nellie and I shared another shrug.

"They found photos of August with Dr. Cason and Burl Botowski," Nadine said. Then she added, "Separately, not all together," and blushed. "Anyway, that confirms the rumors that have been circulating for a couple of days about Burl. It's funny how gossip so often turns out to be true."

I hoped she was being ironic but noticed that Pete and Betina glanced at Nellie with admiration. Breaking a major story in the Teasen and Pleasen was an award-worthy accomplishment, especially when it generated drama with a chain saw and (incidentally) turns out to be true. Pete gave Nellie a thumbs-up. Nellie couldn't help smiling. I was sure that the smile was about relief that her boys hadn't been revealed as the source of this "gossip."

Nadine said that the laptop also contained a list of evil deeds that Annie had perpetrated. "Chief Tanner has a printout of this list," Nadine told us. "Next to most of the items on the list Annie put notes about seeing or talking with the victims afterward. She seemed to be boasting to herself about the suffering she caused."

Nadine recounted some of the entries, which included details such as the look on Mr. Keshian's face when Annie told him that "it must be terrible to know that people in town didn't like him." Annie had also described the things she'd done to Dr. Cason's patients. "She was one sick puppy," Nadine concluded.

After Nadine left, as people in the salon talked about the murder, for the first time some of them were willing to say out loud that they thought Annie had it coming. Everyone still wanted to know who had done the deed, but it was hard to tell if they wanted this person caught or congratulated.

A lot of the talk centered on Dr. Cason as the murderer, now that his relationship with August was known. It seemed obvious to some that Dr. Cason killed Annie because she was blackmailing him and harming his patients. Others pointed out that a doctor's murder weapon of choice was always going to be a syringe rather than a thirty-ought-six. "Maybe he used a rifle to throw us off the scent," shouted one woman who was getting her hair blow-dried.

Betina was certain that the doctor had had an affair with Annie before August came along. When Dr. Cason threw over Annie for August, Annie was jealous, and that's when she began to behave badly, prompting him to kill her. It was therefore all Dr. Cason's fault. Or Annie had been the one to spurn Dr. Cason for another lover, so *he* was the jealous party and that's why he killed her. Again, Dr. Cason's fault.

Someone protested that Annie was clearly the bad guy in this story. Why blame the doctor?

Nellie, who was rather put out with Dr. Cason after seeing the photos of him playing doctor with August, was inclined to agree with Betina that Dr. Cason was at the root of the situation. When Betina heard this, she stopped clipping hair and looked hard at Nellie, trying to figure out what the trick was. Nellie ignored her and went on to speculate that the doctor could have been cheating his patients or health insurance companies as well as cavorting with August. Annie discovered all these infractions, and he shut her up.

Dolores Pettigrew, who had returned for a cupcake, proposed that the doctor had a secret crush on Annie but had never dared act on his desires. He used August as a substitute young woman to fulfill his fantasies, but at last his analytical medical mind couldn't cope with the hurt emotions caused by the yawning gulf between him and Annie, so he did the only thing he could to close the gulf — or, specifically, as Dolores put it, "stop the yawning."

This is a concise version of Dolores' theory. As her discourse unfolded, most people in the salon wondered when the yawning might stop. It didn't help that the rain had returned, dampening the energy of the morning.

To help curb the yawning, other people offered embellishments to the Dr. Cason theories. I didn't really believe that he was a murderer, but I pointed out that Annie was in charge of administration for the doctor. She might have been committing insurance fraud or embezzling from the medical accounts. These offenses made the doctor snap.

As this discussion rambled on, I thought more about the financial angles. The revelations about Annie's evil deeds had made revenge seem the most likely motive for murder. Revelations of August's affairs had made jealousy seem a strong possibility. But what if it all came down to money?

This line of thought brought me back to Rudy's granddaddy. His motive for murder would have been basically about money. Well, that and staying out of jail for moonshining.

Pinning down the revenge motive or the jealousy motive seemed speculative, but the money angle could be checked. Did Annie have more money in her bank account than she should have? Did August have payments coming into her account that were not from her job at the Grosri? I was sure that Woodley would do this kind of checking. How could I get him to tell me what he'd found?

I felt like the money theory was a useful line of inquiry that would definitely clinch the case, until I realized that it wasn't. Even if everybody had been blackmailing and defrauding everybody else, it didn't mean that any of them had killed Annie over it.

The Knockemstiff landscape was crowded with people who had motivations to kill Annie. Only one person pulled the trigger. Who had been willing to do it?

Late in the afternoon, Bee Jameson came in to get her nails done. She brought little Sarah with her. Sarah also wanted to get her nails done, explaining that she and her mother would be performing at open mic that night.

While Nellie was working on Bee's manicure, Sarah was allowed to have one cupcake. When Bee's manicure was done, Nellie asked Sarah what they would be performing that night.

"We will be performing a Broadway song and dance routine," Sarah said. She raised her arms in the air and sashayed back and forth. Pete said that looked like a good routine.

"Do you know about Broadway?" Sarah asked. "My daddy says they call it Broadway because it's done by a bunch of broads."

"Oh, Sarah," Pete started. And stopped. How do you explain politically incorrect language to a six-year-old?

"Pete," I said, "you can try the 'Nice young ladies don't talk that way' approach, although I haven't gotten much traction with that."

"Lester sets a bad example for Sarah almost every time he opens his mouth," observed Bee.

"I know it's a bad example, Mama," Sarah said. "I try to set a good example for Daddy. I think he's improving."

Bee just said, "Ummm," and asked if Sarah could stay in the salon while Bee got some things at the Grosri. Sarah pointed out that she still needed to get her nails done anyway, and Nellie assured a doubtful-looking Bee that Sarah would get the special six-year-old rate.

"Six-and-a-half," Sarah corrected.

"Six-and-a-half-year-old rate," Nellie said.

As she worked on Sarah's nails, Nellie asked, "So you think your daddy's language is improving?" Sarah nodded, entranced by the manicure.

"Does that mean he's not using bad words as much?" Nellie asked.

"I haven't noticed *that*," Sarah said, "but when he goes to swearing nowadays, he tends to do it more in complete sentences."

"That's a good start," Pete said.

"Yes," Sarah said. "I try to encourage him. When he says something to Mama like, 'Damn. You and that woman,' I say, What Daddy means is that he does not approve of you spending so much time with Annie Simmerson. And Daddy says, 'Thank you for clarifying that Sarah.' And then the next time Daddy complains about Miz Simmerson, I hear him say to Mama, 'I do not approve of you spending so much damn time with Annie Simmerson."

When nobody said anything, Sarah looked up at Nellie and said, "See, he used a complete sentence. That's good, isn't it?"

"Excellent," Nellie confirmed.

"Sarah," I ventured, "*did* your mama spend a lot of time with Annie Simmerson?"

"It seemed that way to me," she said. "And to Daddy, obviously."

I think we were all racking our brains trying to figure out a way to ask what Bee and Annie were spending all that time doing. Pete gave up and asked what Sarah and her mama would be singing at open mic. Sarah named a couple of tunes from *South Pacific*.

"That's going way back," said Pete.

"Mama says that's what people like in New Orleans — classic tunes. She thinks we'll be very popular. We'll be NOLA belles!"

We were all wondering if Lester Jameson was in on this New Orleans plan when Bee returned. Sarah did her Broadway sashay for her mother, this time waving her hands with her newly painted nails facing out. Then they sashayed out of the salon. Bee opened her umbrella, and they skipped down Clifton Street singing "Singing in the Rain."

Chapter 18

When our late lunch time rolled around, I decided to go home for lunch. I had an extra hour after lunch until my next haircut appointment and I needed a break. When I came out of the salon, Dolores Pettigrew was across the street holding her umbrella way up over her head with one hand and her cell phone high in the air in the other hand facing east.

"Can you understand me now?" she shouted at the phone. I heard something garbled from the phone. "Oh, I know I'm breaking up," Dolores said. "You're breaking up too. I'll say it three times. Maybe one will go through, dear. What? I said I know..."

I got in my car and drove home, thinking about cell phones, and I had an idea about one cell phone in particular. I parked in my driveway, got out with my umbrella and walked back out my driveway to Tennessee Street. Then I turned down the narrow lane that ran along the side of my lot. This was a dirt track that turned to mud when it rained, and it was very muddy today.

I squelched along in the shallowest patches of mud I could see, wishing I had thought of doing this when it hadn't been so wet or had at least put on boots. On the night I had seen Annie here, we had had thunderstorms that day and for several days before, and the lane would have been quite muddy. Annie must have been determined to get back here with her phone.

When I got to the mulberry tree, I stood under it for a moment, listening to the big drops coming off the tree thunking onto my umbrella. I remembered how as a little girl I loved to walk in the rain in my yellow raincoat, listening to the sound of my own voice loud in my ears inside the yellow canvas "helmet," and the rain drops pattering on me. A couple of crows landed in the mulberry tree, cawing, and shook loose a torrent of drops that cascaded down the leaves.

I didn't see Annie's phone anywhere around the base of the tree, but the leaves under the tree had obviously been trampled on repeatedly over a period of time. Either deer had been lying here or a person had stood here a number of times and probably paced around.

After a few minutes of searching through the tall grass and shrubbery on the south side of the tree, there it was, a dim black rectangle under an ancient holly tree. I reached carefully through the scratchy leaves, past the red berries, and retrieved the phone. It was in a rubberized case, wet. Was it too wet to work? The battery was probably dead.

I did one of the few things I know how to do on a smart phone: held down the ON button. The phone started. After a few seconds it beeped and displayed a message that the battery was low. Yeah, yeah, I thought and tapped the message. It went away, and I was looking at rows of choices. What did I do now?

Give the phone to Woodley, said a little voice in my head. It was the voice of my sixth-grade teacher, Mr. Delouche. "Yeah, yeah," I said out loud. "Eventually."

I looked for a "contacts" icon. I remembered that from the few times I'd used my cell phone before I gave up on it. I found the icon and tapped. The contacts list seemed to be empty. I dragged my finger down the little screen.

Finally, at the very end of the contacts list, I found a single entry labeled "Zero" and pressed it. I could hear the person's phone ringing. I was calling the one contact on the phone of a murdered woman. What did I think I was doing?

The ringing was interrupted by a faint click. I heard a voice say, "Hello" with a heavy Irish accent.

"Connor!" I said. "It's you!" But my voice sounded weird, like I was a robot in an outer space movie.

Connor said, "You? It can't be you! You're dead!"

"Connor!" I said again, louder, as if shouting would clarify the situation. My voice still sounded weird. The phone beeped to tell me the battery was low. "Damn!" I said in frustration. I was about to say that this was Savannah when the phone went dark.

I put the phone in my purse and tramped back up the lane, not being careful where I stepped, mud sucking at my feet with every step. I opened my car door and sat in the seat, and it wasn't until I swung my feet in that I noticed they were balls of mud. That must be why my feet were cold, I reasoned.

I shoved the mud aside so I could unlace my shoes and left them by the driveway. I used the green garden hose to wash off my feet. With the water from the hose making my feet colder than they'd been already, I noted to myself that I'd been about to drive to Connor's. Was this a good idea?

What would a good idea look like at the moment? Would I know one if I saw it?

The only idea I could get going right now was that my feet were cold, so I went in the house and stood in the bath tub with hot water pouring in. I thought about Betina crouching in her tub for safety. That seemed like a good idea. I could just stay here for the rest of the day.

By the time my feet warmed up, I was hungry. By the time I'd had some lunch, I was sure that I didn't want to drive out to Connor's. I wanted to talk to somebody. I put on a pair of boots.

When I got to the salon, Nellie was almost done with her after-lunch client. I walked past her into the back room, saying, "When you're done there, I have an inventory question for you." I sat down at the little desk, wishing I'd got a cup of coffee on my way, but I didn't want to chat with any of the people in the café area.

I went through the mail that was in a little stack on the desk. What was taking Nellie so long? I'd been sitting there for two minutes already. I stood up and spent another minute straightening stacks of towels. Still standing, I went through the mail again. I found my letter opener and slit open each envelope. I threw away one item that looked like a bill but turned out to be junk mail. I stacked the bills back on the desk and sat down again.

I was about to go out to find Nellie when she came in the door backwards, saying, "So not tonight. Bye."

"Nellie!" I said.

She turned around. "Savannah!" she said. "Good news! Rudy called to say they got the license for the distillery. It's all legal. We're no longer felons! Well," she revised, "not on as many counts. Rudy is going by the Tickfaw campground to get the boys this afternoon and bring them home."

Hanging on the edge of my own news, I must have looked dumbfounded at hearing Nellie's news.

"Isn't that great?" she asked. She tilted her head, looking at me in some doubt. "Have you had your open mic beer early?"

"Nellie, sorry. Good news. Great news!" I picked up the stack of bills and straightened it on the desk, laid them back down. "Yes." I stood up.

Nellie sat down. "What's up?" she asked.

I sat back down. "Phone," I said, pulling the smart phone out of my purse. "Found Annie's phone."

"Ah." She tilted her head at me again, knowing there was more. "And?"

"I turned it on and found one contact. I called that, and Connor answered."

"Connor was the only number she had entered in the phone."

"Right," I said. "And when I spoke into the phone, I could hear my voice on the line sounding like a weird roboty voice, like a science fiction movie. You know?"

"Dale had a toy that sounded like that when he talked into it. Drove me nuts. I finally held it underwater until it stopped working. Anyway, did you have a roboty chat with Connor?"

"He thought it was Annie. He said, 'It can't be you. You're dead.' The phone went dead just after that."

"Let's see," Nellie said. "What do we make of this? Annie was calling Connor and disguising her voice?"

"Yeah, so that would be just another piece of mischief. Except why only Connor?"

"Nobody has mentioned getting calls from Annie, have they?" Nellie observed.

"Nadine said that Annie threatened Old Man Feazel," I remembered. "Threatened his dog. How did Annie deliver those threats? Hey," I said. "Annie also poisoned Connor's dog. He didn't tell me anything about getting threats, but maybe Annie used the phone to threaten him using the robot voice. It's scary."

"So he didn't know who was threatening him. That was Annie's usual way of working, wasn't it? She tormented people and watched the results without giving herself away."

"When Connor told me about his dog, he knew it was Annie who poisoned him," I said. "But that was after Annie was killed. So really the only news here is that Annie went to a lot of trouble to call Connor on the phone with a disguised voice."

"It's not *that* hard to get a cell phone," Nellie pointed out.

"But surely it's hard to hide the fact that you've got one," I said. "Woodley didn't know that Annie had a cell phone until I told him I'd seen her with one."

"He should have found out about it by looking at the bills and whatnot they took out of her house," Nellie said.

"Exactly," I said. "And Annie was using the phone behind the far end of my garden, which she could only get to down that muddy nameless lane that runs by my house. That's half a mile from her house. She had to really want to get to that spot, and from the looks of the ground there, she'd stood there a lot."

"All just for Connor?" Nellie said.

"What's so special about Connor?" I wondered.

"August," Nellie said.

"So!" I said, excited by a sudden thought. I grabbed one of the bills on the desk and found a pen. "What if we draw a line between Connor and August?" I drew a line on the back of the envelope.

"We have to draw the line somewhere," she said.

I put a C at one end and an A at the other and wrote "Waycross" on the line.

"Ah, the line is a road."

"Why didn't we think of this before? Anybody going between Connor's and August's would use Waycross Road, not Tennessee Street." I drew another line roughly parallel to Waycross Road and put Ten. on it for Tennessee Street.

"Since the lane by your house connects between Tennessee and Waycross, interior designers might call it a unifying element," she said.

"You've been watching that channel again."

"With the boys away, I've had time on my hands. Can't watch cartoons with Dale all evening." She looked at her watch and stood up. "Speaking of which, I've got one more head to color, and then I need to see what kind of food I can rustle up."

"Your boys will be starved." I didn't want to keep her, but one more part of the puzzle was pressing on me. "I just wonder," I said, standing up, "about Annie being killed on Tennessee Street. Does that mean it has nothing to do with the comings and goings of Connor and Annie? Or does it mean the 'unifying element' is involved?"

"Since we know Annie was sometimes standing halfway along the 'unifying element'? If that lane was paved, you could get to Connor's in a jiffy and ask him if he can explain it."

I opened the door and we filed out of the back room. "I need to give the cell phone to Woodley. Maybe they'll find other info on there."

***

But I was relieved to see that Woodley was not attending open mic this week. I had told him that our delta blues guy, Leander, never came two weeks in a row, which was mostly true. Close enough: it turned out to be true this week.

Something about the phone made me sure that Connor had killed Annie, even though I couldn't put my finger on why, and being sure that Connor was a murderer made me feel terrible. I didn't want to think that Connor could possibly be a murderer. I certainly didn't want to be *sure* Connor was a murderer. And I was reluctant to let Woodley find out anything about Connor.

Connor's *thing* with August still stung, and yet I could not let go of my fondness for him. Which made me feel stupid. Especially if he was a murderer.

At the Knockemback Tavern, Betina said it didn't look like her date was going to show and asked if she could sit at the table with my friend Alicia and me. It took me a second to realize that Betina meant her "date" Woodley and another second to realize that calling Woodley her date was a joke even to Betina. By the time I said Betina was welcome to sit with Alicia and me, my hesitation had said, "No," and it took a while to sort this out.

Misunderstandings like this make me crazy, even if they're funny in the end. The three of us had fun talking trash about Woodley.

Whenever we had kids performing at open mic, they got to go first so they could get home by their bedtime. We hadn't had many kids the previous week because most parents had not wanted to be out with their kids two days after the murder. In retrospect, it was surprising that so many adults had come out that night. Or maybe it wasn't so surprising. People wanted to be with people.

The first act this week was five brothers and sisters who acted out the story of Brier Rabbit and the tar baby, which was originally a Louisiana folk tale before that fellow from Georgia, Joel Chandler Harris, got hold of it. The youngest sibling was wrapped in black fabric to play the tar baby. This was not a speaking role, of course, but the other siblings were energized with a sense of dramatic theater and punched the tar baby pretty hard, resulting in a cry of "owww" each time.

Betina, Alicia and I tried hard not to laugh. Three punches into the play the mother stage-whispered that the older siblings had better take it easy on the youngest if they knew what was good for them.

The second act was Bee and Sarah doing their Broadway numbers to musical accompaniment on a boom box. Bee was wearing her new red dress, and Sarah had on a red dress, too. Sarah danced back and forth, holding her hands out so that everyone could admire her beautiful scarlet nails.

After that we moved on to the usual folk guitarists and accordion players. The three of us at our table sang along (badly) and clapped with one of the zydeco guys.

And then there was Connor. He began by reading a poem that he didn't write, which was unusual. Connor said, "This is 'The Song of Wandering Aengus' by William Butler Yeats, who was an Irishman and a wanderer like myself." Then he read in his thick Irish accent:

I went out to the hazel wood,

Because a fire was in my head,

And cut and peeled a hazel wand,

And hooked a berry to a thread;
And when white moths were on the wing,
And moth-like stars were flickering out,
I dropped the berry in a stream
And caught a little silver trout.

When I had laid it on the floor
I went to blow the fire a-flame,
But something rustled on the floor,
And someone called me by my name:
It had become a glimmering girl
With apple blossom in her hair
Who called me by my name and ran
And faded through the brightening air.

Though I am old with wandering
Through hollow and hilly lands,
I will find out where she has gone,
And kiss her lips and take her hands;
And walk among long dappled grass,
And pluck till time and times are done,
The silver apples of the moon,
The golden apples of the sun.

I tend to be more literal than I should be, but it seemed to me that Connor must see August as the glimmering girl. Connor seemed entranced by August. Was that the same as obsessed? And as the poem suggested, did he not know where August was? I had suspected that he knew where she was all along, that she might even be hiding at his house, that he might be hiding a murderer.

I was so busy thinking, I missed the beginning of his next poem. It took me a while to realize that it was about Finnegan.

So I open my portfolio, and pages of doggerel skew out

With their slurry of little black marks that prompt the eye to wonder what they could be about.

Finnegan would rather I roll up these pages

And throw them like a stick that carries more than meaning, more than ideas for the ages.

What is the value of a life lived here?

Of a moment in time? A week or a year?

Whatever the worth my friend Finnegan may fit,

If you threaten his life, I'll kill you to save it.

He has no interest in my meanings and sentences.

There's only this moment, and love, and its consequences.

The audience in the tavern applauded politely, as they usually did. Connor was well liked, and everyone enjoyed his Irish delivery, but I don't think many people followed his meaning. I wasn't sure I often did.

In this case, I knew that Finnegan was his dog. How many people knew that? Like a lot of people in this part of the country, Connor took his hound wherever he went, but he usually called the dog Fin. And with his Irish accent, I wondered if anyone else in the tavern understood what he had just said. I wondered if I understood what he had just said.

Betina was applauding, and then she noticed that I wasn't. "Did you not like that one?" she asked me.

"It was fine," I said mechanically. I told her I had to go to the little room. I tipped our little round table as I stood up, and Alicia steadied it.

"Did you have a second beer when I wasn't looking?" she asked.

"I've had enough," I told her. I walked outside and looked around. Connor was gone. The only other person out there was Dolores Pettigrew, once again shouting into her cell phone.

I'd walked over from the salon, so I started walking back that way. Light rain was coming down steadily. I didn't notice until my hair was wet and cold, and then I remembered I was carrying an umbrella and put it up.

When I got to my car, I put my hand on the door handle and felt the cool, wet metal. I let my hand drop and stood there thinking about how confusing everything was. Thoughts seemed to be zinging around my brain as if they had a life of their own, and none of the thoughts got along with any of the other thoughts.

I walked down Clifton Street, past Mr. Keshian's shop, past Botowski Hardware. Someone was at the bank's ATM across the street. What did they need cash for at this time of night? I went around the corner and stood under the awning of an antique store, looking in the window at a rusty sled, barely visible in the faint light from another shop. How had that sled come to Knockemstiff? I turned around and wondered how all of these buildings had come to be here, each built by a person who was trying to get something out of life, make money, probably raise a family, leave something to their children. Had they been happy with it all when they were done?

I walked back around the corner and up Clifton Street. When I got near the salon where my car was parked, I saw the familiar dark figure near the salon door. He must have seen me walking this way from the tavern. What did I say to him?

"Tell me you didn't do it," I called to him. "Tell me you didn't."

"I didn't do it," he said, only he didn't say it with an Irish accent. It was Woodley.

"Uhh!" I said. I didn't know whether to be relieved it wasn't Connor or peeved it was Woodley, except that I was definitely peeved it was Woodley.

"Nice to see you, too," he said. "By 'it,' you mean murder Annie Simmerson?"

"Something like that," I said in a feeble effort at running the other way.

"Let's see, what's *like* murdering Annie Simmerson? Murdering August Anderson?"

"That's not funny, really," I objected. "Especially if you're saying that August has been murdered."

"Wish I knew."

If he had been wanting to find out if I knew, I guess I'd told him I didn't.

"Investigator Woodley, before you ask, let me tell you that I don't know who killed anybody. I have suspicions that I won't tell you about, if you can live with that."

"I learned long ago to ignore amateur theories," he said to my huge annoyance. He was trying to offend me.

"We amateurs only get in the way, I'm sure." I walked over to my car. "Have you been following me?"

"No, no, I was out walking and saw you go down the street. I figured you'd end up back here at your car, and I'd say hello."

After you'd frightened me by lurking here, I thought. I promised myself I'd install an outside light and opened my car door.

"Oh, I almost forgot," I said. "I have something for you that I found earlier today. I'm sure it's nothing." I walked over and handed him Annie's cell phone. "I found it at the spot I told you about, where I saw Annie using a cell phone? For some reason, your professional law enforcement people missed it."

Then I got in my little amateur car and drove away.

Chapter 19

Friday, end of the week: I was usually glad to see the weekend, but as this Friday morning dawned murky and still raining, I had an uneasy feeling about what I needed to do. Like any sensible person, I put it off as long as I could.

My first idea had been to drive over to Connor's first thing and get it over with. I'd demand to know whether he'd killed Annie. He'd answer yes or no. Then he'd kill me. Or he wouldn't.

Although I felt uneasy about this confrontation, I didn't feel afraid because Connor didn't seem like a murderous person. And yet I was going to ask him if he had murdered someone.

I'd never asked a person whether they'd murdered someone before. There was probably a technique to it that the professionals used. Maybe the best approach was to get the person chatting about other things that had nothing to do with murder — Lousy weather we're having, The price of sorghum is down this week, Did you hear that Bee Jameson is running off to New Orleans? — and then pause offhandedly and say, *Oh, by the by, did you kill that awful woman?*

Sitting at my kitchen table eating a bowl of cereal, sipping at a cup of coffee, milk, no sugar, I pictured myself having this conversation with the murderer. I decided to go into the salon to make sure everything was good for the day there. I had a 9:30 and then nothing after that until almost noon. I'd drive out to Connor's then. I could go down Waycross Road, see what everything looked like from that angle.

As I parked in front of the salon, I thought about Woodley and the phone. Would he call the Zero contact in the phone and frighten Connor again? And would Woodley be able to tell that I'd done that yesterday? Woodley might want to talk to me about that. Whatever. While he was at it, he could thank me for finding the phone.

As I unlocked the salon door, a little blonde six-and-a-half-year-old person appeared at my elbow. "Good morning, Miz Jefferies," she said.

"Sarah, good morning. What brings you out on this rainy day?"

"Mama asked could I get my hair cut this morning," she said.

"I'm sure you can," I said looking her over. She was wearing the red dress I'd seen her in at open mic the night before. "Didn't you get your hair cut last week? You're not exactly desperate for a cut with a capital D."

"Mama is the one with the capital D. That's what she said last night."

"Last night after your open mic performance? That was very good, by the way."

"Thank you, Miz Jefferies. I wish Daddy had been there to see it. He was busy having one of his 'Damn' days."

"Why don't you go ahead and get up in the chair, Sarah. I think I can trim your hair before my 9:30 gets here."

"I guess that's the way Daddy takes care of business," she said, climbing into the chair. "Everything is damn with a capital D."

"Well, we need not worry about that," I said.

"I suppose you're right," Sarah said. "Mama worries about it some. That's why she was using the capital D last night when she and Daddy were discussing her red dress again. 'I'm done with you with a capital D,' she told him. I went out in the yard and took a nap."

"In the rain?"

"I have a tarp."

We talked about the weather then and whether they were having the same weather in New Orleans. Nellie came in and said that all her boys were back home at last, and the house was back to its usual chaos. Sarah observed that Nellie's boys were wild animals, so living in her house must be like living outdoors. Nellie allowed as how that was true.

"Fun," Sarah said. "And you don't even need a tarp."

Nellie told me that since she had seen Aubrey and Norris earlier in the week, they had discovered more photos on Annie's laptop.

"Who was August with this time?" I asked, glancing down at the little blonde person in my chair.

"Nobody," she said. "They were the same photos they had found of Burl and Dr. Cason, only with a different woman — a different woman's face, anyway."

"I'm totally confused," I said. I wondered if Nellie was leaving out stuff that she didn't want to say in front of Sarah.

"What happened was that Annie had the photos of Burl and Dr. Cason, and she Photoshopped August's face into the photos. That's the word they used, 'Photoshopped.'"

"That's a picture-editing program," Sarah explained.

"So Annie edited the pictures to make it look like August was, ah, involved."

"Apparently," Nellie said. "So August was only half as involved with her flower child activities as we thought."

Nellie was telling me what Rudy had said about the new distillery when Woodley came in. He began by thanking me for discovering Annie's phone. He said it was curious that the phone had one number in it and that was for Connor — whom he was on his way to speak with — and that someone had used the phone to call that number yesterday.

"Some amateur?" I suggested.

While he was thinking of a follow-up question, he recognized the little person in my chair and asked her if she'd brought her thirty-ought-six.

"Not today," Sarah said. "Daddy told me he needed it."

"Has he gone hunting?" Woodley asked. "Nothing's in season, is it?"

"I believe you're right about that, Investigator Woodley," Sarah said. "He just said he needed it and ran off."

Woodley took a professional interest in people running off with guns. "Sounds like he's in a hurry to do some target shooting," he said.

"I'd hate to be one of those targets today," Sarah said, "since he's having a 'Damn' day."

"That's a day when the only thing he says is 'Damn' all day," I explained.

"You never know what might cause a 'Damn' day," Sarah observed, "although it often involves some activity of Mama's. That's probably the case today, since she went to check out some things in New Orleans. When I mentioned it to Daddy, he got all excited."

Woodley gave me a startled look with a question in it, as if I might know what Lester Jameson might be thinking of doing with that thirty-ought-six. I gave back his startled questioning look with a little shrug, and he rushed out the door.

I told Sarah that Nellie would finish the last of her trim and then find her a treat in the café area.

"You're not going after Bee?" Nellie asked.

"No, I have another errand to run before Woodley gets around to it."

"Connor? Are you sure you want to go there?"

"No," I said. "I just have to."

"I'd offer to go with you, but somebody has to stay with Miss Sarah," Nellie said with the clear meaning that she wasn't about to go see the man who could be the murderer.

I'd driven out Waycross Road many times but never with eyes for murder. If the killer had come along here, what did he or she see? Why was the killer carrying a rifle? Was he or she hunting Annie? Or did this person just happen to see Annie and just happen to be carrying the rifle and happen to have a reason to chase her down and shoot her?

When I got to the point where the nameless lane — the "unifying element" — intersected Waycross Road, I pulled over and looked down the lane toward the mulberry tree. The area along here was sparsely wooded, and I could easily see the mulberry tree. Annie may have felt as though she was hidden in the darkness underneath that tree, but the light from the phone's screen would show her face to anyone coming along Waycross Road, just as I had seen her from Tennessee Street.

I drove on to Connor's. He was at his forge on the side of his house. He looked up as I pulled into the drive and then went back to hammering the white-hot metal he held with a pair of tongs. He kept at his hammering as I walked up to the forge.

"Hey Connor."

"Hey Savannah."

I watched him hammer the metal. His blue T-shirt was plastered to his body with sweat, and his wild red hair and beard shuddered with every clanging blow of his hammer.

"Watcha making?" I asked.

"A poem," he said.

He turned the metal and hammered it. Held it up, turned it, hammered.

"It's as Blake said," and he hammered the cadence as he recited:

Here alone I in books formed of metals

Have written the secrets of wisdom

The secrets of dark contemplation

He held the metal up, put it back on the anvil and hammered:

One command, one joy, one desire,

One curse, one weight, one measure,

One King, one God, one Law.

He held up the metal and then plunged it into a trough of water. The steam hid his face. He put down the hammer and tongs.

"Would you like a cup of tea?" he asked, wiping his face with a towel.

August was in the kitchen, and Finnegan came up to me as I came through the door.

"Finnegan, you look all better!" I crouched down and ran my hands along both sides of his long-eared head. He wagged the rear third of his body.

August was wearing jeans and a T-shirt rather than some exotic outfit — a little disappointing. But I was so happy to see her alive that I almost cried. She told me she had fully recovered, thanks to Connor. She'd been sick in bed for most of the past couple of weeks.

Connor was making tea. I apologized for scaring him with the call from Annie's phone.

"Gave me quite a shock, it did," he said. "After I had time to get my wits about me, I decided the police must have found the phone."

"So Annie was threatening to poison Finnegan using that weird voice, so you didn't know who it was?"

"I'd get a call almost every day. I didn't take it too seriously at first, but then somebody left poisoned hamburger meat outside the house. Finnegan must not have cared for the taste of the stuff, because he didn't eat much of it. What he did eat made him pitiful sick. You saw how he was."

August put cups out for us, and Connor set the teapot on the table.

"Then I heard that Old Man Feazel's dog'd been poisoned. I kept getting the threatening calls. About that time August had the allergic reaction. She was in the other room there struggling to breathe. I was going more than a little crazy with all this, as you might imagine."

He poured tea in the cups.

"So you went to August's and got her rifle?" I asked.

"I felt like I had to defend my castle, you know? I didn't know who I might be dealing with, but I knew it was someone cruel. I've never thought of shooting another human being, but I wanted to shoot whoever was threatening Finnegan, a poor creature who couldn't defend himself."

"Did you walk to get the gun?" I asked.

"Yes, I don't know why. I didn't want my truck seen at August's. I didn't want to deal with Sanders."

"And you saw Annie under the mulberry tree."

"Didn't recognize her at first, but I was suspicious of somebody sneaking around out there with a cell phone." He stared into his tea. "When I got closer, I heard that weird voice and knew I'd found the person who was tormenting me. I confronted her, and she ran out to your street. I followed her and caught her there. She told me August was a slut. She told me she would come back and finish off Finnegan and finish off August."

He looked up at me. "So I shot her."

August put her hand on his arm.

"Now I need to find that Woodley fellow and quit all this," he said.

Chapter 20

Knockemstiff has not quite returned to normal yet. We need a new doctor and some highly principled people will not do business with Burl Botowski.

But I'm walking to the salon again on days when the weather is fine. Sometimes Sarah and Finnegan walk with me to the salon. Sometimes I drop both of them off at Mrs. Chabert's.

Because Connor was instrumental in saving the lives of several patients whom Annie was gradually killing with bogus prescriptions, the judge gave him a lenient sentence. It turned out that Dr. Cason had indeed been defrauding insurance companies, so he lost his license and is doing some jail time.

August moved to San Francisco but found that all the flower children had moved south to a town on the coast called Santa Cruz. Before she could move there, August fell in love with a software billionaire and married him within a couple of weeks.

Woodley hasn't located the Jamesons yet, so Sarah has been living with me along with Finnegan. Sometimes we weed the garden and talk crow-talk with the crows that perch on the fence until Finnegan barks at them and they fly away. Sometimes I hold Sarah up so she can pick mulberries from the mulberry tree. And sometimes Woodley shows up and we have lunch at the Bacon Up. At least he's gotten rid of that wrinkled sports coat.

Thanks for reading!

You can find all of my books by visiting my Author Page.

Sign up for Constance Barker's New Releases Newsletter where you can find out when my next book is coming out and for special discounted pricing.

Sign up to be a part of my ARC Team. You'll receive a free copy of my newest release in exchange for a review on Amazon.

I never share or sell your email.

Visit me on Facebook and give me feedback on the characters and their stories.

These books are all from my Caesars Creek Series

A Frozen Scoop of Murder (Caesars Creek Mystery Series Book One)

Death by Chocolate Sundae (Caesars Creek Mystery Series Book Two)

Soft Serve Secrets (Caesars Creek Mystery Series Book Three)

Ice Cream You Scream (Caesars Creek Mystery Series Book Four)

Double Dip Dilemma (Caesars Creek Mystery Series Book Five)

Melted Memories (Caesars Creek Mystery Series Book Six)

Triple Dip Debacle(Caesars Creek Mystery Series Book Seven)

Whipped Wedding Woes(Caesars Creek Mystery Series Book Eight)

A Sprinkle of Tropical Trouble(Caesars Creek Mystery Series Book Nine)

A Drizzle of Deception(Caesars Creek Mystery Series Book Ten)

Sweet Home Mystery Series

Creamed at the Coffee Cabana (Sweet Home Mystery Series Book One)

A Caffeinated Crunch (Sweet Home Mystery Series Book Two)

A Frothy Fiasco (Sweet Home Mystery Series Book Three)

Punked by the Pumpkin(Sweet Home Mystery Series Book Four)

Peppermint Pandemonium(Sweet Home Mystery Series Book Five)

Expresso Messo(Sweet Home Mystery Series Book Six)

Whispering Pines Mystery Series

A Sinister Slice of Murder (Whispering Pines Mystery Series Book One)

Sanctum of Shadows (Whispering Pines Mystery Series Book Two)

Curse of the Bloodstone Arrow (Whispering Pines Mystery Series Book Three)

Mad River Mystery Series

A Wicked Whack

A Prickly Predicament

Eden Patterson: Ghost Whisper Series

The Mystery of the Courthouse Calamity

The Mystery of the Screaming Elms

The Mystery of the Morbid Moans

The Mystery of the Ominous Opera House

Witchy Women of Coven Grove

The Witching on the Wall

A Witching Well of Magic

Witching the Night Away

Witching There's Another Way

Made in the USA
Middletown, DE
09 May 2017